The Boxman: An Epic Saga

Peter D. Rusatsky
Copyright 2019

Prelude

The Back Story

Around June 1996 my wife Debbie, daughter Kimberly and I travelled 250 miles to attend Mass at Saint Maximillian Kolbe Church in Scarborough Maine. The purpose of this journey would require another short novel. Suffice to say it was a very important reason. Here's what happened.

As we walked down the aisle, something jumped out at me. There was just one other person in the Church, a twenty something or so, young woman, already sitting about four rows from the altar. We had arrived early since we didn't know what times Masses were. Not too many people arrive that early for Mass, so I took notice of that. We sat just a few rows further back, on the opposite side of the aisle, but in very close proximity to the young woman.

This Mass was like none other. Not due to the Mass itself, but due to the young woman who had my keystone. During the entire Mass, I was acutely aware of this young woman. So much so, that something was gnawing at me the entire time. I kept saying to myself, chill out. There was absolutely no reason, whatsoever, that I could explain what was happening as I continuously glanced at her. I had not and could not see her face. There was not a single reason for me to be drawn to her. She did nothing to draw anyone's attention; she wasn't crying, or anything else. Completely inconspicuous to everyone but me.

So..., Mass ended, and we struck up a conversation with someone behind us. We hadn't ventured into the aisle but a few feet from our pew. That conversation lasted about five minutes. I was about to receive my keystone. When the conversation ended, I turned towards the altar and immediately noticed the young woman still sitting in her seat, the only soul left in the Church besides us. I was overwhelmed by the thought to go to her. I remembered feeling very uncomfortable about that. This is not something that came naturally to me, especially since I did not have my keystone. I've spent over 23 years now, getting emotional every time I think of her. And so, without my keystone, I did what I have always done and turned to walk out of Church with my family. I was the last in our little procession down the aisle and out of Church. Neither Debbie nor Kimberly was aware that I walked about twenty feet and stopped. Full stop! I turned around, not knowing, I was about to receive my Keystone, and my life permanently altered. I did not deserve what I was about to receive. The young woman had no idea I was now walking towards her as her back was to me. She was seated as close to the aisle as could be. It wasn't two seconds before I knelt at her side and said the heaven-sent words.

Are you O.K.?"

Well, my world changed in a heartbeat.

She looked at me and...tears exploded out of her eyes. She kept looking directly into my eyes and said nothing. My Keystone arrived as I was holding her hands, while kneeling in the aisle. Tears cascading out of her eyes as she did nothing to wipe them, all the while holding my hands. The keystone moment arrived when I watched and felt the river of tears falling off her chin, onto our hands. I was in a new world. I looked her in the eyes and promised her, I'd pray for her.

She never said a word. Total silence!

Even the tears were silent.

By now, Debbie and Kimberly had seen what was happening and had returned near me. As, "coincidence" would have it, I said to my daughter, "Kimberly, give me that Walkman tape". The tape was a recording of a onetime spiritual concert recorded just several months prior in Stratford, Ct. I said to the young woman, I have something for you and placed it in her hands. Again, I told her I'd pray for her and kept that promise for over 23 years now and will continue to do so. And so, it was at that moment I realized...

"People have big problems... all people"

Are you that young woman?

As of 2019 you'd be about 43 years old. I'm guessing you were about twenty years old then. If you recognize this story and you are that young woman, please contact me at, boxman.epic.saga-@gmail.com. I'd be thrilled to meet you again.

You became the inspiration for "The Boxman: An Epic Saga"

Dear readers, this novel is based upon fictional characters and events. However, the settings are very real. It takes place primarily on the Campus of Salve Regina University in the City of Newport, Rhode Island, USA. The preceding link captures most of the buildings in this novel. The links throughout the novel will help envelop readers in the magnificence of the historic Victorian and modern grandeur of Salve Regina University. **Links to buildings throughout the story have "Photo Galleries" which give readers an amazing portal into the story!** Other notable locations are

Lauralton Hall in Milford, Connecticut and American School for the Deaf in West Hartford, Connecticut.

The Governor's Ball is real. See Ochre Court, as it plays a prominent role in the novel. The novel's cover picture is that building. Refer to links as the story progresses. ***Also, follow the music video links of important songs that are an integral part of your journey. Turn the volume up!!! Hearing those songs will draw you into the story in a profound way.***

This story contains a "River of Tears".

You may shed your own?

But in the end...in the end, they all come to dry!!!

Fasten your seat belts...the journey begins!

"The Boxman: An Epic Saga"

Uh-oh!

(Dawn) Go to hell you god damn psycho!

(Stevie) Fuck you asshole!

(Dawn) You're gonna rot in hell you son of a bitch.

*(Dawn) I swear to God ...You'll
pay you son of a bitch.*

...this is the little Stevie remembers about that day. What was to come of that verbal onslaught and the next few milliseconds would change his life forever. All the demons in his life had conspired to come together in a symphony, in one moment in time. In a conspiracy, brought upon him by himself.

On that sunny fall September day, in Newport Rhode Island, on America's Cup Avenue, something ultra-serious had occurred. Looking back, that day had been in the makings for years. There had already been similar days, at different places and times.

The venom that spawned his vile behavior was already intertwined with his spirit.

He came to Salve Regina University that year, as a seasoned psychopathic piranha, a social misfit in all things but one. Stevie could play football... really well! His arrival here would spell doom for the smaller fish. He'd rip their flesh like he'd always done. What he didn't rip, he'd devour like a flesh-eating bacterium. Either way, the result would be the same, until today. This day, a petite young woman would rattle the fabric of his existence. His epiphany would occur. "Space Time Compression" would nearly cost him his life!

Here began his "Keystone" journey. Today that petite young woman would lose control of an entire lifetime's worth of "Self-Control". She'd **"strike"** him, in such a way, that the earth's axis would tilt, if just for a nano second.

Today, he sought out the Deaf girl, again! But today, a bill came due! Not that he had any idea at the time... but a big bill came due! He did not have the "Funds" to pay but pay he did

Chapter one

They were always together those two. Marcie the Deaf girl and Dawn the Deaf girl's roommate. They were both nursing students at Salve Regina University in Newport Rhode Island. Most just call it "Salve". It was a matter of necessity that Marcie and Dawn be together as much as possible. Since they were both in the Nursing program, Dawn was Marcie's official interpreter. She stood at the head of every class along with the Professor. The notes that Marcie took were their co-possessions. After four years together in high school, Dawn had mastered American Sign Language (ASL). Now was their fifth year together, having met as freshmen at Lauralton Hall. Lauralton Hall, the all girls' high school Academy in Milford, the oldest Catholic girl's high school in Connecticut. Marcie couldn't help but stand out her first day of freshman year at Lauralton since she was the only one to show up with an interpreter. Having scored exceptionally high on the difficult entrance exam of The Academy of Mercy, as Lauralton Hall is otherwise known, they had to find a way to accommodate this talented young woman. Certainly, Lauralton had their share of special needs students over its 100+ year history, but this was their first profoundly Deaf student. An academy such as this, with walls exuding the Works of Mercy, would surely find a way. Marcie did not have a problem with the entrance exam since it was all written. As a matter of fact, she didn't even stand out the day of the exam. So, there was really no heads up that day. Marcie preferred it that way since she never liked being the center of attention because she was Deaf.

She especially didn't want to stand out or be a distraction that day! As it was, Lauralton's entrance exam was known to be extremely difficult. By default, it must be able to separate out distinguished academic talent. The academy's rigorous academic program is not for the faint of heart. As is every year, there are always more applicants than there are seats in freshman class.

And so, Marcie received her acceptance letter as did Dawn. But now, the academy had to be told.

So, on that first day of class, everyone would meet the Deaf girl, including Dawn, since they had been placed in the same home room. Word spread like wildfire that not only was there a Deaf girl, but also a male interpreter in his twenties. The girls were instantly enamored with him. Dawn was immediately struck by the fact that the interpreter was not deaf himself and did not read lips. Why did he learn sign? Turns out he had a Deaf sister. Even though Marcie could read lips, she could not read the teacher's lips and take notes at the same time. Furthermore, great lip readers can only decipher about thirty percent of spoken words. Her interpreter knew to pause as Marcie took notes and to resume as she looked up. Greg had been an outstanding student himself but became fascinated by the curriculum of the Academy. After each day's classes he would meet with Marcie's teachers to discuss things he may have missed or things he may not have understood himself. There was one issue the Academy was unable to overcome and that was the fast pace of lectures. The Academy's main goal was to prepare talented young women for college and demanding careers beyond. They could not alter the fast pace of the academics. So it was, that first day at the Academy.

Although many girls this age are *"unspeaking"* around their parents, Dawn could not help but to discuss every detail of the Deaf girl with her parents that night. In his usual form, Dawn's dad listened intently to all she could share that night. He was known to take in large volumes of information and respond in an unbelievably brief way. Often, perhaps most times, it was in the form of a question. And the answer to that question was one he didn't necessarily expect an answer to right then and there. Honestly, he didn't necessarily expect a verbal answer at all. And so, in his classic way, his question to Dawn was...

"and what can you do to help her?"

Dawn did not necessarily understand her father's wisdom, and it often angered her that he would seldom give her the answer she sought.

But always, she'd come back to the question at a later day and time and replay it in her mind. This time however, time was not on her side as her thoughts swam.

In homeroom the next morning she asked Greg to introduce her to Marcie. As the other girls watched, Greg began signing to Marcie that Dawn wished to be introduced to her. Through Greg, the two discussed where they were from, the grammar schools they attended and how they came to attend Lauralton Hall. Dawn learned that Marcie was from Shelton Connecticut and took the train to school.

This was so typical, since the train station was practically across the street from Lauralton Hall. For this reason, Lauralton could cast its net for talented young women farther than most schools. Girl's anywhere along Metro North's Southern Connecticut corridor from Greenwich to New Haven and areas north through the "Valley" could hop the train to Lauralton's doorstep. The Lauralton girls in their Catholic School uniforms were a common sight on the rails as were the boys on their way to Fairfield Prep, an all-boys Catholic high school in Fairfield. Though separated by ten miles or so, they are thought of as brother-sister schools. Prep, a Jesuit school and Lauralton a Sister of Mercy school. Dawn learned through Greg that Marcie passed through the Stratford train station on her way to school each day. Bingo! That was the most valuable piece of information that Dawn could possibly have gained that day. Though every girl from this area knew about Shelton and most had probably been there, few girls if any would have known its compass direction from Stratford. Dawn was no better informed of Shelton's actual location, than before this little conversation. The truly meaningful fact was, Marcie's journey from Shelton Ct. to Milford Ct., somehow intersected Stratford and that was all she needed to know. Marcie learned that Dawn was from Stratford, a town adjacent to Milford and that Dawn had attended a well-known Catholic grammar school by the name of Saint James. As luck would have it, Dawn practically lived in Saint James' backyard and had walked to school for years. That mattered for nothing right now.

The thought that totally occupied Dawn's teenage brain now, and for the rest of the day, was the Stratford train station. It was literally a quarter mile from Saint James and three blocks from her house. This thought, so occupied her teenage brain, that she didn't notice the teacher enter the room and ask the Lauralton Ladies to take their seats. And so, with Greg to the teacher's side the rigors of Lauralton academics for the next four years had begun.

Dawn's parents had planned that Dad would drop her off on his way to work each morning and Mom, or some other Stratford mom, would deliver her home. It was the same plan for most girls who didn't ride the train. All of that would change as far as Dawn was concerned. At lunch that day, Dawn, with Greg's assistance, would query Marcie, as to how you go about riding the train. As Dawn would find out, you took your Lauralton I.D. to a Station like Bridgeport, that was a full-service station, and you purchased a discounted month-long train pass. Amen!

Dawn was practically salivating like a rabid dog as a bold new teenage plan evolved in her brain. It would not be unusual for a Lauralton girl to hatch such an impromptu plan that involved such mental gymnastics. This is what Lauralton girls did. That's why they were at Lauralton in the first place. The goal of the Academy is to teach talented young women to think and prepare for college. And prepare they do. The colleges these Lauralton Ladies are accepted to are literally a who's-who of the finest colleges this country offers. It all begins with minds like Dawn's and Marcie's that run as fast as a greyhound.

Young women this age speak at two speeds, either nineteen to the dozen, or not at all. If, it is not at all, and you ask them a question, the most likely response will be "fine". If you're lucky and get the other option, no matter what you ask them, you'll get a lengthy lightning fast reply. So fast that nineteen words will leave their mouth in the same time that normal people can speak twelve.

Mind you, it's not that they are not "normal" teenagers, but these teens grew up with the internet and as a result even their manner of speech has been amplified to a new speed, even for teenagers. Fortunately, they can understand each other perfectly well. It's only parents and other dinosaurs who can't decipher, "nineteen to the dozen". Well, being the second day of school, Dawn's mom was sure to pick her up that day. With great trepidation she dared to ask Dawn how it went. With typical anxiety as to how she would reply, Mom got more than she anticipated. Nineteen to the dozen came spewing from Dawn's mouth. As fast as words can fly, Dawn spurted out, "Mom, where is the Bridgeport train station?" For obvious reasons, Dawn's mom was caught by surprise. They were still in the line to exit Lauralton Hall as Mom tried to rationalize this question. Dawn had already anticipated this and launched into the following explanation. Mom... since the train practically passes by our house on the way to Lauralton it would be so much easier on you and dad if I took the train. To mom's great amazement this made some sense since she worked a part time job and Dad headed opposite his job to drop her off in the morning. And so, in twenty minutes or so Dawn was in the concrete chasm of the Bridgeport train station where she proudly paid for her month-long pass. Dawn was kind enough to share some other tidbits about the day but never mentioned the Deaf girl. Little did her Mom know, while waiting for Dawn to purchase her pass, that she had unknowingly played a part in her daughter's life that would have profound implications for Dawn and many others.

As a matter of fact, that little pass is the starting point for the rest of Dawn's life.

As is typical of teenagers and especially Lauralton teens, Dawn's mind had not sat idle for one second that day and was not sitting idle right now. It was no surprise to Dawn that her teachers had assigned homework on the second day since she was well aware of the extremely fast pace and challenging curriculum of Lauralton. There was this junior high teacher at Saint James School who had the highest regard for Lauralton and its rigorous academics since her own daughter had gone there.

Mrs. D. took keen interest in students in her seventh and eighth grade classes who possessed the mental and spiritual qualities that could benefit from and survive the intense rigors of that kind of curriculum. When Mrs. D identified these young women, she would encourage them and their parents to seriously consider Lauralton Hall. Dawn was one of the students who Mrs. D selected each year to attend a science competition for junior high school girls held on a single Saturday each year at Lauralton. These young women, usually four or five, compete against teams of girls from many area schools both near and far. These young women become keenly aware of what Lauralton expects of them having competed in this event. They also become aware that there are many other young women that are as equally talented as themselves. Mrs.D also makes it clear, that there are more applicants to Lauralton than there are seats. So ...having passed the entrance exam for Lauralton and submitted a significant essay it came to pass, that both Dawn and Marcie vaulted the first high hurdle of Lauralton Hall... getting in the door!

As Dawn plunged into her homework that second evening, she had one teenage thought on her mind. Getting it done and getting on the internet. So as 9:00 rolled around she hurriedly opened her laptop, her mind on the two simple words she'd type into her search engine. She was so fixated on the outcome of that search that she did something unfathomable for a teen her age. That evening, she had no contact whatsoever, with any of her friends either by cell, internet, or any other way. As is typical of teens her age, born into the digital age, their fingers move faster than their thoughts. As she typed "sine language" and hit search, for a millisecond, her mind could not grasp the results. When her mind had an additional 3 milliseconds to catch up to her fingers, she realized her mistake. Flying over the keys she correctly entered "sign language" and hit enter. She let out a long breath, since she had waited all day to see that page. For the next hour she feverously learned two simple sentences and fell asleep after signing them repeatedly.

Chapter Two

Metro North, Stratford Train Station. Most people nowadays have become somewhat conditioned to people seemingly talking out loud to themselves. There was a time when heads used to turn, because at one time, talking out loud to oneself in public, was probably a sign that something was not quite right. Even though most people are quite considerate of the afflictions of others, especially mental ones, the human mind tends to look at things it senses are unusual. But, insofar as people talking to oneself in public is concerned, we've conditioned our minds, like Pavlov's dogs, to completely ignore such a stimulus. We now know, with near certainty, that our neighbor is on a cell phone or Bluetooth and our mind only takes momentary notice, perceiving no threat and sending no signal for any type of bodily reaction, except perhaps, an uncontrollable sense of annoyance. But that conditioning process holds true only for certain stimuli that we are exposed to, over and over, that the mind eventually learns to ignore. The people on the train platform that morning simply could not ignore this new stimulus to which they were being exposed. As the train began approaching and all were facing its arrival, it was obvious that nearly everyone was looking at the girl from Lauralton in her characteristic jumper. She was talking to herself but not out loud. Her hands were moving a mile a minute and no sounds could be heard. Sign language, is a stimulus our minds are simply not able to ignore. Why? It is a unique kind of stimulus that's not threatening but intriguing. A stimulus that is so fascinating to "hearing" persons that our minds are inherently enamored by it. Our minds can't process both its simplicity and complexity at the same time. The mind is also drawn to feelings of compassion. Dawn had positioned herself at the end of the platform where the last car of the train would stop. Since the train was further in length than the platform, the conductor would overshoot the platform by several cars so that the last car was adjacent the end of the platform. This way, should the cars be full or close to full, those entering would begin to walk towards the front of the train for a seat. So, that's how it was, that everyone's eyes were on Dawn. As the train arrived and she faced the void of the rails below her, hands and fingers and arms were flailing wildly. Not a single passenger the length of the platform could ignore this stimulus.

When the squealing of the air brakes had concluded and the doors opened five seconds later, Dawn was a person on a mission. She immediately entered the car, stopped, and began to scan the entire car for Marcie. When she realized she was not there, she raced through the car, seemingly possessed, till she entered the next. So, it went for five more cars. For those not familiar with the stops along Metro North's corridor, it's important to know that the Milford stop for Lauralton Hall is the very next stop after Stratford, about six minutes. Dawn had to execute her mission with urgency. Her plan was to find Marcie and communicate two sentences in six minutes or less. Marcie was facing the front of the train… *and did not see Dawn approaching.*

When she was at Marcie's side, she tapped her on the shoulder and stood resolutely in the aisle. And there, the first communication of their lifetime together unfolded. In nearly flawless "sign" Dawn said, "How are you today Marcie?" Dawn's sign of

M-A-R-C-I-E was exceptionally good. So good, that Marcie understood her perfectly and answered her "great". Dawn of course had no idea what Marcie had just signed to her, and so, she let fly her next salvo of words which were "Can I sit with you the rest of the way?" When Marcie replied "of course", Dawn again had no clue, but had assumed all along that Marcie would say yes and instinctively sat next to her. Marcie's mind raced. She remembered Dawn from the previous day but could not understand why Dawn had not signed to her since she "obviously" knew sign. It was also confusing to Marcie that Dawn had a blank look on her face as she signed to her. As the train was already pulling into Milford, the two exited the train and down the stairs to street level. Now, all the Lauralton girls on that train were fixated on Dawn and Marcie. Dawn finally had the presence of mind to stop, pull out her cell phone, type something and show it to Marcie. When Marcie read it, she had a broad smile and shook her head affirmatively. The message said "Marcie... I don't know sign". Dawn had no way of knowing that Marcie could read lips or that it was even possible. I just learned those two sentences online last night. I wanted to be able to talk to you this morning." The rest of the day they exchanged text messages.

Dawn explained in detail how she convinced her mother to let her ride the train, how she learned to sign online and how she hoped Marcie would teach her sign. Dawn texted, "I want to be your friend" and Marcie replied, "I'd like that very much." It is true that cell phones have had enormous effect on the Deaf's ability to communicate with others. It was also true, that Marcie's closest friends were also Deaf and had attended school for the deaf together for many years. They didn't rely on technology to communicate. Marcie's mind raced as she imagined that, for the first time in her life, someone other than her parents wanted to learn her language, in order to be her friend.

Both girls texted their parents that they would be late getting home. As far as the trains were concerned that was never an issue. Metro-North trains never seemed to stop. Since Dawn lived three blocks from the station, that made life very easy for her as far as her trip home was concerned. Marcie had to put a little more effort into her planning since she lived a mile from the station. Not that it's an insurmountable distance to walk, but you must figure in weather, and the fact that, Lauralton girls usually have half the Library of Congress in their backpacks. Marcie had to give her parents some clue as to her arrival time. So it was, that sign language classes began that very day. They agreed to meet in the Mansion, and they sat on the bottom step of the sacred staircase that the girls were forbidden to use for access to the second floor of the Academy. For obvious reasons they were as quiet as a mouse. Marcie decided to start with the alphabet.

Even though Marcie could read lips quite well, she felt it would be better for Dawn not to know this and therefore not be able to use it as a crutch. Part of the curriculum was that Dawn could not speak during the lessons. Questions went via text. Marcie instinctively knew that if Dawn was to enter the Deaf and "cannot speak community", she'd need to leave her comfortable world of hearing and speaking behind, at least for now. There are medical/psychological reasons why a Deaf person either cannot speak or chooses not to. The word mute is a term that can be interpreted as offensive and is preferably replaced by "cannot speak". They only made it to the letter F that day. You could see the passion in both girl's faces as Marcie signed a letter and Dawn repeated it over and over again until Marcie saw complete success. When Marcie felt that success had been achieved, she'd move on to the next letter. Each time a letter was added she'd begin to sign the previous letters in random order to test Dawns recall. Eventually she began to string letters together randomly. It might seem like two hours would be a long time to learn to sign six letters, but by the end of that first lesson Dawn was signing F_A_C_B_E_D and then D_E_B_A_C_F and each time the pace of Marcie's signs increased. Learning sign is a two-way street. It's not enough to be able to perform the sign; you must be able to read the sign as well. To Marcie this was just a natural way to teach Dawn since sign was the only means of communication she ever knew. Marcie's parents were quick to pick up on her deafness, as they realized she never responded to any audible clues such as the sound of a rattle or any other audible toy. So, teaching sign was not anything Marcie had to

think about. As far as she was concerned, she was just teaching Dawn her language. Something that was as natural to her as anyone else speaking in their native tongue. Although Marcie was profoundly deaf and did not typically speak, she did have the ability to make out some very loud sounds including the beats of very loud music, especially bass sounds and loud environmental cues such as car horns, fire alarms, etc. Deaf persons develop an ability to "feel" loud vibrations in their body especially in the breastbone area. For that reason, Marcie had been taking dance lessons from a very early age. Provisions had to be made for Marcie to wear headphones, since the necessary volume without headphones, would far exceed the sound level others could tolerate. In addition to her headphones a speaker was pointed directly at her with sound absorbing foam on the wall. She could hear deep base notes but relied, more and more, on her ability to "feel" the vibrations of the music. Having made all the necessary accommodations for Marcie, she fit in with the rest of the troupe and everyone accepted her with very little notice that she was somehow different. This became so important to Marcie, to be able to hear "something", that her dancing quickly became noticeably different than others. Others danced to the audible beat, but ...

Marcie "felt" the beats as if in rapture!

This rapture was extremely noticeable. Parents who were able to come and watch their children during class, could not help but focus in on Marcie. She was very different in her dance.

As caring parents do, both asked how the third day of school went. Marcie gleamed as she signed to her parents all that had happened. Dawn answered "fine".

When asked why she was late getting home she said, "I joined a club". What kind her dad asked. "Language". He realized she was not engaging in conversation and left it as such. Dawn offered up only one more morsel..., "We meet every day!"

As the days began to pass Dawn found herself focusing more and more on Greg as he faithfully signed in the classroom. By now, the fascination of the girls with Greg had begun to wane. At first you could see that the girls were distracted by Greg's signing and often found it difficult to concentrate on the teacher. Now, it"s as if he wasn't even there. That was true for all the girl's but one. Literally every day, Dawn could seemingly understand more and more of Greg's signing. Not that she understood much, but when he would spell a word for Marcie, Dawn could often be seen to smile, because her recognition of these fast flying letters was getting better and better. By now, Marcie and Dawn had completed the alphabet and Marcie was convinced she could throw any combination at Dawn and she could clearly understand and fluently repeat them. The truth was, that she had such a keen fascination with sign, she was acquiring the language at breakneck speed. It didn't hurt that Dawn had always been a straight "A" student at Saint James and scored extremely high on Lauralton's entrance exam. She was one of those gifted learners who had now acquired an addiction for a new language. Something was about to change though. It happened because of "Meet the Teachers Night" at the Academy. This is the night that Lauralton parents follow the schedule of their daughters, attending their classes and meeting their teachers. It's done in the evening, each class fifteen minutes or so. Just enough time for teachers to present a short syllabus, express their expectations and answer some questions. The girls would be home as usual…studying.

Everything was proceeding normally for Dawn's parents until they arrived in her Spanish class. At the end of the period Dawn's mom raised her hand to ask a question. Since Dawn had joined a language club, and she assumed it was Spanish, she asked the teacher to share something about the Club. She mentioned to the Spanish teacher that it must be a wonderful club for her daughter to stay every day after school. At first the teacher was confused. She knew that Dawn was not in the Spanish club and that it only met twice a week. Dawn's parents were intrigued that she would even commit so much to a scholastic club. Dawn had always been a high achiever in sports, especially basketball and softball, and one additional "sport" that was the most important to her, having started in third grade. It was an unspoken curiosity of Dawn's parents that since school had started; she never once spoke about sports. Dawn's parents did not care one way or another whether she played sports but were curious as to why she had such an abrupt loss of interest. Dawn gave up all sports and continued with only one extra-curricular activity, the one she started in third grade. That "Activity" would later have profound consequences! When the teacher realized what was going on, she asked the parents to see her after the "class" ended. You could see a look of concern come over their faces. Since this was the last period of the evening, the teacher asked them if they had a little time to meet with her and the Principal. Dawn's Dad, a man of few words, was now at a complete loss of words. Neither parent had a clue, what could be so important, that a meeting would be necessary with the Principal. The only time any teacher had ever spoken to them was to heap praise on their daughter for her high achievements. Something very different was in the air and they both knew it. They became even more concerned when the Principal arrived. They entered the Principal's office together and sat down. The Principal began by saying how thrilled she was to have Dawn in Lauralton Hall. She was all smiles as were Dawn's parents. They were more like deer in headlights since they could not really focus on the Principal's accolades. They knew something else was going on here which even the Principal did not know... yet. Tensions began to build when they were asked by the Spanish teacher to have a seat outside the Principal's office for a few minutes. For now, they sat on a couch under a beautiful chandelier imagining what their daughter could have possibly done to create such an urgent need for such a meeting and why they hadn't been told something sooner. They both held hands but neither said a word. When the Principal's door reopened, she had a noticeably different look on her face. She invited them in. The Principal quickly assured them that everything was o.k. She began by asking them what Dawn had told them about the Spanish club. Dad spoke up to clarify the fact that Dawn said she had joined a Language Club and they just assumed it was the Spanish Club since that was her language of study. What else did she tell you? Mom replied that the club met every day from two o'clock till four. We kind of thought it was odd for a club to meet every single day, but, like clockwork, she'd arrive home right around five, so we never gave it any thought. Has she ever mentioned any of her new friends at school? Both looked at each other for a second because neither could remember Dawn speaking about any of the girls at school. But just then, Dad, always a keen observer and listener, added something. I remember only once, on the first day of school, Dawn spoke like a bundle of energy about a Deaf girl in her class. I want to say her name was...Marcie? I remember the name because she had so much to tell us about Marcie that she must have said her name twenty times. But that's all we know about her friends here and she has never really spoken about Marcie since.The Principal and Teacher instinctively knew the answer to the parents' concerns. Both were aware of what had been going on after school each day, and had both assumed, that Dawn and Marcie's parents knew as well. Marcie's parents did know, but not Dawn's. The Principal spoke first. She began by saying, you should be very proud of Dawn except for the fact she kept a tiny little detail from you. Dawn did join a language club! From the day they met, Marcie and Dawn have become inseparable.

They're like conjoined twins who were not separated at birth!

Like two animals in a "Yolk". Are you familiar with a Yolk? Both parents said, not really. Your daughter, and all our Lauralton Ladies, will become very familiar with that concept over the next four years. At one time most people were very familiar with a "Yolk" and the spiritual concept of a Yolk. A yolk is a device that connects two animals together. In other words, Marcie and Dawn are now "bound" together. Dawn has developed a passion for learning American Sign Language from Marcie, to become her good friend. This is especially meaningful to Marcie. Marcie attended grammar school at the American School for the Deaf in West Hartford, Connecticut and her lifelong friends have always been from the Deaf Community. ASD has highschool as well but Marcie had heard such great things about Lauralton she decided to give it a try. Truth be told, she had not had a close friend from the Hearing Community. So, every day, for two hours after school, they'd sit in the library, Marcie teaching Dawn her language. We've both been here at Lauralton several years and it is one of the most beautiful things we've ever witnessed. The parents, like those unable to speak, took it all in, said nothing more, and thanked them both for their time. Upon returning home they found Dawn absorbed in her homework. Dawn asked how it went. Mom said, wonderful. We especially enjoyed learning about your Spanish Club and how well you are doing. Dawn looked at them with a queer look. She knew they knew! Her parents said goodnight to her. They could not have been prouder.

So, days, weeks, and months passed, and Dawn was acquiring ASL at an amazing speed. Teachers and staff would pass by the library after school and witness the tenacity Dawn showed for this new gift she was receiving. It was unique to see two persons communicating in total silence. Marcie's lip reading is a skill acquired by only some of the Deaf Community. Only about thirty percent of words can be lip-read even by the most able. The "Reader" must exert immense focus and mental concentration to accomplish this. With only one third of the words being read, the deaf person must quickly fill in the remainder based upon the context of the conversation and taking body language into account as well. It is mentally and physically exhausting. Marcie was not technically, "unable to speak". Having been born, profoundly Deaf, she struggled with speech. Many deaf persons have a difficulty with the volume, pitch and sound of their voices making it difficult for others to understand. Marcie would use speech at home as her parents could understand her perfectly well.

Sometimes...

very emotional moments for Marcie would result in speech.

But for the most part, Marcie remained silent, and

with Dawn, that was almost always the case.

However, ...

the relationship Marcie would have with the Boxman

would include speech!!!

By the end of freshman year, a very significant meeting took place at Lauralton, including Dawn and Marcie, both their parents and all necessary staff. Since precise interpreting would be necessary, Marcie's Mom became that person. All witnessed the flawless signing between Mother, Daughter and Father. Of course, Dad was expert as well. Dawn and Marcie had already been to each other's homes frequently and so all knew each other. Dawn was keenly attentive as Marcie would sign with her parents at home. Hands, arms, fingers moving in perfect harmony. And so, it was decided that Dawn would become her official interpreter at Lauralton. Greg, the young interpreter who everyone had developed a deep affection for, would no longer be needed in that role. He had been a keen, active, supporter of this transition during private conversations with Marcie and Dawn. He could not have been happier for Marcie and Dawn and Greg was especially enamored by the deep friendship Marcie and Dawn had developed.

As the years passed, Dawn's "fluency" increased every day. It was especially important that Dawn acquired exceptional fluency in the terminology of the sciences, such as biology, chemistry and physics. Dawn and Marcie had profound conversations about the future. Dawn had also made several trips with Marcie to visit her close friends and teachers at the American School for the Deaf. It helped Dawn acquire more in-depth skills, signing in a group of persons. It was a result of these trips and conversations that Dawn came to realize that young deaf persons have the same aspirations as others. Those aspirations included a Political Scientist, a Chef and many other occupations. Dawn came to respect these aspirations as no different to the hearing. Dawn also had the privilege of meeting students from far flung places such as Puerto Rico, Thailand, California, Vermont and other states. As you would expect, this world-renowned school, drew a student body from long distances.

Dawn became close to Marcie's parents especially her Dad.

Although neither was deaf, in approximately 70% of cases of genetic hearing loss, the cause is autosomal recessive. A parent may carry one of the recessive genes responsible for deafness while the other copy of that same gene is normal. Because each parent has only one recessive gene that can cause hearing loss, both parents can hear normally. Marcie inherited both recessive genes. It was a unique environment for Dawn, as Marcie sometimes spoke verbally to her parents. Of course, they signed back or Marcie read their lips. Dawn only witnessed this while at Dawn's home and at The American School for the Deaf.

As, God, or luck would have it, both aspired to the same goal. Marcie kept this a secret from all, except Dawn, her parents and friends from ASD. Amazingly enough, both had the same longing even before meeting. Marcie had internal struggles concerning her goal. She was blessed with having been born into the digital age. She knew that it might be possible to succeed in her chosen profession, if..., several "Digital Technologies" could be brought to bear. She was consumed during junior year as to all the digital needs she would have need of, such as Video Phones, and the myriad of communication platforms available to her. She realized it could be possible! She also knew that she'd need to find a college that could help her succeed with this. Since Dawn and Marcie both aspired to the same "High Calling", an "Agreement" had already been reached between the two. That conversation, bound them together in heart, mind, and spirit. In a "yolk" neither would ever abandon. They'd either both succeed, or both fail. Dawn had already agreed to be her interpreter for college. Their mutual "Higher Calling" also explains why both girls had to be profoundly fluent in the terminology of the sciences and medicine.

When the time arrived for preparation and applying to college, Marcie and Dawn always met with their mutual guidance counselor, together. This kind woman was aware of the "Plan". Because of their great admiration of Lauralton Hall and the Sisters of Mercy's Mission, Marcie and Dawn increasingly became more and more focused on a college run by the Sisters of Mercy. This College was aware of the extreme academic rigors of Lauralton Hall Since both girls were at the top of their class it would be a shoo-in for their acceptance. However, one was Deaf.

And so...they applied and wrote their essays only to this one college. This college was originally founded as an all-girl college with only a single curriculum. Today, it has a very diverse range of studies, and is co-ed, but still maintains a prestigious reputation in that field.

Marcie took a chance when submitting her essay. It was supposed to be a minimum number of words, far more than what she wrote. Of course, Dawn professed her expert knowledge of ASL and her relationship with her dear friend Marcie. Neither mentioned the "Plan".

Marcie wrote...

>*"I want to be a "Compassionate" Nurse.*
>
>*I also want to be the first Deaf Nurse to graduate from*
>
>*Salve Regina University!*

PETER RUSATSKY

Both received their acceptance letters.

Chapter Three

During the summer, multiple meetings took place at Salve regarding the "Plan". Those meetings included the President Sister Mathilda, (her professed name), and a Sister of Mercy. Also, multiple faculty members in the Department of Nursing and others, their advisors, and Dawn's parents. Marcie's Mom passed away Junior year of Lauralton which had a devastating effect on Marcie. Now...

Marcie's Dad was sick, very sick.

It should also be noted that Salve sent Marcie her acceptance letter with no contingencies, as that would not be true to the character of the Sisters of Mercy. They'd figure that out later. Salve had a long history, even before laws required so, to make accommodations for persons with unique needs. This was nothing new for them. Marcie's essay had a profound effect on all that read it including Sister. Marcie's essay would not have reached Sister's desk in the normal course of events. Obviously, her essay was very different. What struck the President more than anything else was the particular use of a single word. **"Compassionate"**. Truth be told, we all have some idea of the meaning of "Compassion" and "Mercy". The Lauralton Ladies are well schooled in the meaning of Mercy and the "Works of Mercy".

Both girls knew...Mercy is defined as, "Compassion or forgiveness shown toward someone whom it is within one's power to punish or harm". There it is, the word "Compassion". But what is "Compassion"?

The Lauralton Ladies knew that word has profound meaning. It is **"the willingness to suffer with another"**. That singular word in Marcie's essay did not fall on "deaf" ears.

All the details were worked out. They would of course be roommates in freshman housing called Reefe Hall. Salve Regina University is in Newport Rhode Island. Their "Dorm" room overlooked the "Breakers Mansion" and the Atlantic Ocean! Not too shabby. Salve is ranked as one of the "Fifty Most Beautiful Colleges in America" and eighteenth of the "Most Transformative Colleges in the United States". There's no wonder the girls wound up here.

Chapter Four

Dark clouds on the horizon... and not storm clouds.

The "Piranha" had surfaced.

Everything was going exceptionally well so far, but the god-damn Piranha had surfaced.

Their Professors were simply amazed by the girls. In several weeks' time, the other nursing students had acclimated to the unique class structure, and, like all things, soon found it perfectly normal. Both girls soon became good friends with other Nursing students and were often seen together, especially on Bellevue Avenue, Thames Street and America's Cup Avenue. This was the release mechanism for many students especially nursing students. Modern day nursing school is not for the faint of heart. It is an especially grueling program. It was especially beneficial for the girls and their new friends to walk those historic streets, visit Starbucks, and, eventually return to McKillop Library or their dorms for a late night of study. It was already a very demanding program and clinical rotations hadn't even started. These walks, including banter about the cutest boys were deeply meaningful to all. There were always five or more together.

Newport is home to 25,000 or so residents and 2.5 million or so visitors each year. Aside from the unbelievable beauty, visitors are drawn to the grand historic mansions of the Victorian period. One of those mansions is Ochre Court, the epicenter of Salve University. Salve was originally chartered as a women's nursing college on Aquidneck Island but there was one slight problem. The good Sisters of Mercy did not have land or a building. Just a minor detail. So, a gentleman and his wife by the name of Goelet donated one of the grand mansions of Newport and its furnishings to the good Sisters. That structure housed all the nursing students, the good Sisters, classrooms, everything.

PETER RUSATSKY

The value of that gift in today's dollars would be astronomical. But over all these years, that gift, precipitated thousands of wonderful graduates who have had meaningful impacts in this world.

Early that fall, the Piranha began to harass the girls but especially the Deaf one. The Piranha, whose actual name was Stephen, aka, "Stevie" was already on the administration's radar including the President. He had a history of extremely bad behavior, especially on the football field. If he wasn't hurting or harassing people, he wasn't content. He'd already been thrown out of two games by referees for extreme willful misconduct resulting in injuries to opposing players. The girls had been to a few games, witnessed the behavior, and became acquainted with that vile behavior on and off the field. He was a recognized blemish on the football program and was personally warned by the University President. Where did he learn this vile behavior? Partially from a father, who raised him to win at all costs, no matter what. However, his father was not complicit in Stevie's personal persona of a "Pariah Piranha". This genus and species were Stevie's personal endeavor. Somehow, he escaped scrutiny of the Football recruiting process. This would not last.

Another thing happened that fall, but no one remembers exactly when.

The Boxman first appeared.

There he was in a wheelchair on America's Cup Avenue.

Each day he would appear out of nowhere, take up his same usual place on the sidewalk with a sign attached to his wheelchair, one on each side. They read..., "Free Help". You could tell right away he was not physically well. So, as luck would have it, the Piranha now had two enticing victims, the Boxman and Marcie and any who might be in their company. Stevie had a handful of so-called friends, who typically kept company with him. Maybe out of fear of becoming victims themselves but certainly not out of true friendship or respect. Misery likes company.

Each time he passed by the girls and their friends or the Boxman, insults flew. In the case of Marcie, the insults also included wild hand gestures. Marcie, aware of the taunts, could not hear what he was saying and out of kindness, neither Dawn nor the other girls ever told her. The "Boxman" also received verbal insults and mocking regarding being in a wheelchair although no one called him the "Boxman" yet. As a matter of fact, Stevie gave him that name. Awfully gracious of him. Although Newport Police had Stevie on their radar, the President nor others were aware of the mayhem occurring "Downtown". Dawn, who was always in Marcie's company, became uncontrollably upset with Stevie and on multiple occasions got in his face, to no avail...yet!

And so, the Boxman, sat all day, in the sun, rain, wind, cold and anything else Mother Nature could throw at him. Often the girls would bring him a Starbucks out of genuine compassion. He would nod his head and thank them. The only times he would leave his station was to go to a restaurant's restroom or get a bite to eat. Otherwise, he was there from 8 o'clock or so till four. No one knew where he came from or where he'd go at night. But, every day, seven per week, he was there.

At first, as best as anyone knew, no one stopped for "Free Help". Takes courage to reach out for help, even free help. But on occasion, someone, perhaps two, would seek his help. On top of his wheelchair, across his lap, he carried to and fro a plastic folding chair for his "Guests".

One day, except for a flimsy umbrella, practically useless with the winds coming off the ocean, he was sitting at his station in the pouring rain. The girls stopped and asked him how they could help him. He asked them for a piece of paper and something to write with. His hands shook badly as he wrote and drew a sketch. There appeared to be two boxes, side by side, and he gave them exacting verbal instructions. Since freshman couldn't have cars on campus, they found that they could use the Trolley to get to an appliance store in town. What a look on the part of the trolley driver when they appeared with two refrigerator boxes. They had to remove the top and fold as flat as possible to get them on the trolley. That night, they met in secret in the main entrance of McAuley Hall which they knew would be open late. They were all familiar with this building. So, they re-secured the top of the box with its metal band and completed all the additional architectural work with a box cutter as detailed by the Boxman. The next day, they hand carried, quite a walk, from Reefe Hall to America's Cup. One girl on each end of each box, and their friends, who all switched off along the journey. Like geese fly.

This was later in the afternoon as all had to finish their classes. As would be expected, the Boxman was in his usual place except that there was one person seated and two waiting. They knew full well, how to do the final assembly, as the Boxman described in his previous instructions. When the first "Customer" had finished, they moved their Grand Mansion into place with the Boxman in one box seated in his wheelchair and a two foot by two-foot opening between the two boxes. The other now housed a seating place for those needing help. The Boxman's box was cut away in the front for access with his wheelchair and similar with the other box, except the opening was on the side, so guests would have their backs to passersby and some measure of privacy. A rope, procured by the girls, would wrap around the entire mansion in the evening and secure it to an adjoining rail. Most nights the Boxman struggled to secure his new abode to the fence but more and more often, passersby would help as well. The only architectural detail left was to secure two weatherproof signs the girls had procured from the art department, which were secured one to each box with snap ties, reading, "Free Help". The next guest entered with almost no interruption. People were becoming keenly aware of the Boxman especially Stevie. As luck would have it, Stevie was nowhere to be seen the day of construction. The next day upon seeing the new structure on America's Cup, walked directly up to it, confused by it all, blurted out for all to hear. "Here lies the Boxman". Little did Stevie know, the Boxman would help save his life.

Chapter Five

A little about Marcie and Dawn. When Marcie's parents realized she was Deaf, they were understandably shaken as there was no deafness in either of their families. They immediately undertook an exhaustive study of her condition. They became very familiar with the great debate over Cochlear Implants and decided not to have Marcie "implanted" for reasons that reflected their own education in this field. They committed themselves to profound study, including classes in American Sign Language. That worked quite well for this family. Before long, all were communicating in sign. By sheer luck they lived within commuting distance of The American School for the Deaf, the oldest in the U.S. Marcie had all kinds of intervention in her young years, including speech pathologists, audiologists, her Doctor and instructors in American Sign Language. Her parents brought every resource to bear. When she was four years old, she entered preschool at the American School for the Deaf. They also knew she was not completely deaf. She would react to loud environmental sounds such as car horns and her teachers documented that she did alert to fire drill horns as well. Fire alarm horns also contain strobe lights to alert the Deaf to an emergency. As a result of numerous visits to the American School for the Deaf (ASD), and conversations with other parents, they learned something they would not have anticipated. Deaf people dance! Not only do they dance, they love to dance. This became especially clear when they asked to visit with two of the high school classes. They could both sign, so they did not need an interpreter. They asked lots of questions of a freshman and senior class but were keenly interested in asking students if they danced? These were small class sizes, 5-7 students each, since classroom desks must be arranged in a circle so everyone can see everyone else signing. The hallways of ASD are also wider than normal to accommodate groups of people signing. So, what was their reply to dancing? One hundred percent said they danced.

This was overwhelming news for Marcie's parents. Imagine that. But it gets better. In people who have a profound loss of a sense, other senses are often heightened to help the person acclimate better to their environment. If you asked most hearing people if they can "Feel" music, they would invariably reply, that no, they hear music. But not so, with the profoundly Deaf. If music is loud enough, their bodies can feel music. Amazing. If they can feel vibrations, they can feel the rhythm of music and enjoy music just like hearing people. "The perception of the musical vibrations by the Deaf is likely every bit as real as the equivalent sounds, since they are ultimately processed in the same part of the brain". Wow!

So, armed with this amazing information, next stop was a dance studio. Marcie was four years old. After much discussion with the dance studio, a special speaker was installed, directed as best as could be, in Marcie's direction to shield others from the intense volume. This increased her ability to "feel". She still wore headphones to focus the music to her inner ear. It meant that Marcie was somewhat isolated from the other dancers, but she adapted well. Special sound absorbing material was installed on the wall directly behind Marcie's dance area to help the situation. As with most dance studios, parents often attend to watch their little ones. After only about one-year, other parents began to tell Marcie's, that their daughter had some unique dance talent. Truth be told, it became common for parents to be focused in on Marcie. As the years passed, it became profoundly evident that Marcie had entered a world of her own. Parents were mesmerized by her and every year she had her own solo at the dance recitals. The praise that was heaped upon Marcie, especially after the recitals, was something her parents could not ignore. Marcie could dance. Oh, could she dance! And Ya, Salve has a Dance Minor and a very large Dance Club. "SRU Dance Club"! She had already decided to minor in dance and immediately joined SRU Dance Club. As these circles were out of her comfort zone at Salve, and Dawn did not dance with her, special arrangements, consistent with her former dance school, had to be made in order to accommodate Marcie as best as possible. It became immediately clear to Marcie that she was being warmly welcomed by those in the Dance Minor and SRU Dance and that many happened to be in both. She was very happy with this. For her entire life, Pre-K through Senior in high school, her immediate circle of friends had always been Deaf, excepting Dawn. The environments she was in now, nursing, dance minor, SRU dance were slowly expanding her universe within the hearing community, something that would become necessary in the "hearing profession" of nursing.

It wasn't long, immediately in fact, that one of the

dance professors took notice of Marcie. She was witnessing a level of dance never seen in college age students. It was a level of dance she'd only witnessed once before in her entire career. She texted Marcie one day that she'd like her to come to her office with Dawn. Everyone knew Marcie had a conjoined twin. Otherwise there'd be a lot of texting. The meeting lasted an hour. The professor made her an offer. Something way outside the normal boundaries of the college's curriculum. She offered Marcie private instruction, at no cost. Private instruction was in a sense an oxymoron. It was more a question of who would teach who. This professor was so intrigued by Marcie's dance she had a professional endeavor to see what Marcie was truly capable of. So, they began. Only criteria, Marcie could only call her Katharine. This was all on the QT. Only other person who knew was Dawn. This all took place within two weeks of Marcie's arrival at Salve.

As for Dawn, she had always been a great daughter. She was blessed to have had a wonderful science teacher at her Catholic elementary school in Stratford, Ct. who always encouraged her to pursue the sciences. For all her life she had been very involved in sports. She excelled on the junior varsity and varsity basketball teams in grammar school and was very involved with softball. That all changed when she met Marcie. There was only one extracurricular interest which she began in third grade that she maintained. That would factor into Stevie's epiphany. Little did Stevie know!

Chapter Six

Marcie was asked by Katherine to choose music, she decided upon, as part of their private studies. Without much hesitation, Marcie choose two songs which she really loved, that had enough base and volume for her to feel. She knew all the words from the internet. Katherine was thrilled with her selections. She loved those songs as well. In no time, other dancers would stay and watch Marcie's private classes as everyone was enthralled and awe stricken by her dance. Word spread about this, and it wasn't long before Sister Mathilda appeared at the door to watch. She had overheard people talking about the Deaf Girl. They were all saying, have you seen her dance! As it was, Dawn and Marcie frequently met with Sister Mathilda to touch base on how things were going in Nursing. She had not known anything about "Dance". For no other reason, she was intrigued to find out what everyone was talking about. Katherine saw her standing at the door with others. When Sister witnessed Marcie's dancing, she was simply fascinated. She'd never seen anything like it. Upon leaving, she summoned Katherine to her office the next morning. They hatched a "plan" and Sister Mathilda thanked Katherine for all she was doing with Marcie.

Things were coming to a boil for Stevie. His verbal onslaughts directed against Marcie and the Boxman increased in magnitude and frequency though this never reached the ears of Sister Mathilda. He somehow remained under the radar of the Football Program especially after his first and final warning from Sister Mathilda. Sister made it clear; the cost of any further discipline was expulsion. This couldn't happen as far as Stevie was concerned. Stevie wasn't an unusually big player, actually, on the thin side. The perfect physique. He was very intelligent to boot. Only problem... he was violent. This was not consistent with his major of Criminal Justice as he was in fact a criminal of sorts already.

The lines were growing longer. Now people were waiting up to three hours to see the Boxman. Word had begun to circulate, that he was in fact dispensing "Free Help" to people, many of whom were at their breaking point. But Stevie was not fazed in the least by the people in line. With more and more conviction he always blurted at the top of his lungs, "Here lies the Boxman". The reason word was spreading on campus, as well as elsewhere, is that several Salve students had visited the Boxman. Also, a news reporter wrote an article in the local newspaper and with the internet it went viral. The article was titled, "Free Help". One thing that became very clear, by observation and firsthand testimony was that the Boxman very rarely spoke. People would describe heart breaking problems, very often in tears, to him. Every time, he could be seen to be in great thought while listening to strangers' problems and could often be seen with his head in his hands as if in prayer. Unlike Marcie, his sense of hearing was very good. He was a very keen listener. He was a very keen listener.

Since the Boxman's box was completely visible to the outside, unlike the "Guests" box, people would often stand near him and observe and wonder. One thing that became abundantly clear from observation and testimony was that every person left with a smile and a newfound spring in their step. They kind of danced out of their "meeting".

Truth be told, there was one person who did not leave with a smile or a spring in his step. Everyone in town knew who he was. He was the owner of the mega yacht, frequently docked in Newport. Locals observed him standing in line one day. Of course, the Boxman did not know him and it would not have mattered. He sat with the Boxman for over an hour. There were two specific things that were part of the Boxman's good counsel. No matter the severity of someone's problems, his approach was the same. His hallmark included enormous concern, reflection and compassion. He could be seen to look directly into that person's eyes and soul and say two to three sentences to that person. Then, he'd extend one hand and place it on that person's head and say the exact same thing.

"Be good to yourself and others".

It's not clear why that soul left unrelieved but that would come to be known at a future time.

All good things eventually reached the ears of Sister Mathilda, and the Boxman was no exception. She had her fingers on the pulse of all things Salve and all things Newport. Shortly thereafter she was seen in line with many others. Many Salve students observed this as everyone knew who she was. Eventually she entered the box and sat in the plastic folding chair. The Boxman said, hello Sister Mathilda. You know me? I do Sister, but we have never met. They held hands the entire time. Sister Matilda had practiced the "Works of Mercy" her entire life. She could see he was very sick. She asked him where he was staying and who was taking care of him. He told her. She left after deep conversation with the same blessing as all the others. He only said one sentence to her before her blessing. "I believe you will be receiving a special visitor before long"

Chapter Seven

Salvation will come to this house... today!

Stevie's epiphany would fall on this date.

Marcie often asked the others what Stevie was

saying, and they'd never tell her. Dawn's fuse was getting shorter and shorter. She became more and more agitated and had confronted Stevie, face to face, on several occasions. One of those outbursts on the part of Dawn and Stevie went like this:

(Dawn) Go to hell you god damn psycho!

(Stevie) Fuck you asshole!

(Dawn) You're gonna rot in hell you son of a bitch.

(Dawn) I swear to God ...You'll
pay you son of a bitch.

Today would have a very different ending. Today, justice would come to Salve and Marcie and the Boxman. It wasn't the form of justice that would be espoused at Salve, but justice, nonetheless. In his typical fashion, Stevie crossed paths with the Deaf girl and her friends including Dawn. And of course, the same taunts. Stevie was across the street but could be seen and heard by all. Dawn disappeared into an altered universe. For all her training in self-control, since third grade, she could not control herself now. That training would not help her now. She blacked out. She heard nothing and saw nothing... except Stevie. So much so, a car had to skid to avoid hitting her as she crossed the street. Stevie saw her coming as did his small entourage. He assumed it would be like his previous encounters with her. Dawn was a petite young woman about half Stevie's size. That didn't matter now, as Dawn had temporarily left this universe. A few steps later they were face to face. Stevie went to say something, but the words never came out of his mouth.

She would "strike" with the lethality of a Green Mamba!

A leg flew out of nowhere and anyone within thirty feet heard a loud crack. Stevie was out cold, sprawled on the sidewalk. Dawn turned and walked away. When the Police and ambulance arrived, he was still out cold and for a moment his friends didn't know if he was breathing, but he was. The story his friends told to the Police and emergency room doctor was that Stevie tripped and smashed his face on the sidewalk. The doctor could not reconcile that with the severity of his injuries. His jaw was broken clean through. What was the one and only extracurricular activity that Dawn continued in, since third grade even after giving up sports? Why, that would be Brazilian Jiu Jitsu, exceptional for self-defense, because size doesn't matter. She was a third-degree black belt!

The wildfire spread uncontrolled, other Salve students witnessed the whole event. Not more than 24 hours passed that the entire student body didn't know what really happened. Both Marcie and Dawn received a text, the very next morning to immediately report to Sister Mathilda. And with great trepidation they did. Sister was very calm. She asked them if they witnessed an incident on Avenue of America's Cup the day before. Dawn spoke for both. She answered, yes, we did. Do you believe it had a good outcome? Uh... yes, we do.

O.K. then girls, you are dismissed. No one ever looked at Dawn the same way.

Now, Stevie disappeared for two days, word had it, he was still in Newport Hospital. One thing's for sure. The Campus was alive with gossip. Everywhere Marcie and Dawn went, they noticed people talking and pointing in their direction as if to say...that's her. Both girls were taking it in stride. Dawn had re-entered this universe about an hour after taming the shrew. So much harm had been done to the girls by Stevie, there was relief in knowing that it was now all over. Marcie and Dawn chose to skip breakfast this day as they still had systems full of adrenaline. But as lunch approached, they decided to go to the main dining venue in Miley Hall. As they walked up the four interior steps, they suddenly heard the volume of the cafeteria go from very high to zero, as soon as they walked through the main doors. Of course, Marcie couldn't hear the change in volume, but she could see every single head turn. The volume only crept up incrementally as all eyes were focused on the two, now getting their food. They sat down with their other Nursing friends and one by one they gave Marcie and Dawn high-fives. They had all seen what happened but decided to keep a low profile that evening. Two Policemen suddenly walked in and scanned the room for Dawn having secured her picture from Campus Security. They were already very familiar with what happened to Stevie, but he couldn't talk. His jaw was wired shut. I guess you'd say he was suddenly, "unable to speak".

Now you could hear a pin drop. One of the officers asked Dawn if she knew what happened to Stevie the previous day. I did see Stevie on the sidewalk, and I heard others say he tripped and fell on his face. Did you go over to Stevie at any time? Yes, but I could see he needed immediate medical attention and others were already calling. This same Officer then kneeled next to Dawn so that only she could hear. He looked at her very directly and said a few things, and both Officers left. Marcie immediately signed to Dawn, "Are we going to jail?" ... "What did he say?". Only Dawn knew what Marcie had just signed. Dawn answered her, in sign only, as she did not want anyone else to know. The first thing the Officer said to me was, you know we've had a significant problem with a boy named Stevie for some time now. Are you aware of that? Yes, I am. The next thing he "whispered" to me was, "thanks for solving this little problem for us". We didn't have the "resources" to remedy the problem so quickly. He smiled and winked at me. Now they consumed their lunch like hyenas, and everything was right with the Universe.

The Earth was back on its proper axis and the cafeteria volume went back to normal. However, one other little thing occurred. Several of Stevie's hyena friends had just placed their empty trays on the moving belt and were leaving the cafeteria. One of the three broke from the others and headed straight toward Dawn. He bent down and said, I speak for all of us..., "Nice job", loud enough that all the girls heard. Then, he rubbed her on the head before leaving. All realized there were three less hyenas in this world.

As for Stevie, paramedics had been keen to check his airway, as blows to the jaw can also cause other life-threatening injuries. They radioed the hospital to prepare for "trauma victim". They were told to administer oxygen. Stevie was writhing in pain. He did regain consciousness while being treated on sidewalk. Upon entering the emergency room suite, he was immediately taken for a CAT scan to look for intracranial bleeding and to evaluate the extent of the fracture which would dictate his treatment. As luck would have it, Stevie's mandible break was clean through and radiology showed there were no other cracks. This would avoid major reconstructive surgery. As it was, his jaw required intermaxillary multiple loop wiring, i.e., wiring his jaw shut, so the crack could heal. The oral surgeon agreed with the attending emergency room surgeon. They were befuddled by the fact that, jaws can be broken by trip and falls, when the person cannot react in time to break the fall with their hands. But, in Stevie's case, the soft tissue damage to his face was way more consistent with a high velocity impact. They noted as such in his chart but had to rely upon the "testimony" from his friends who described the incident as a fall. Either way, Stevie had no idea what had happened. His last conscious recollection was seeing Dawn crossing the road. Nothing more, nothing since. He would find out soon.

On the third day, Stevie reappeared, and was first seen by all in Miley Hall. No one was with him and his gaze was continually downward. They all realized he could not speak, and his cheek area was still discolored, black and blue, and very swollen. He was now on a liquid diet consisting of milkshake concoctions of all types. He found the furthest unoccupied table and could be seen trying to sip his nourishment through a straw. Those within good eyesight saw what appeared to be braces in his mouth. Only hideous. His former hyena friends were all at another table and refrained from joining him. Stevie did already know what happened. It was two days after the incident when he was discharged and returned to his dorm room in Young Building by Uber. No one saw him return as all were in classes. Later his roommate appeared, one of the former hyenas. Stevie still didn't know what happened. All he knew was what the doctors said his friends witnessed. Neither spoke for about five minutes. Stevie was still on pain killers. **Unable to speak, he wrote on a piece of paper,**

"What happened to me?"

(High volume response heard by others outside their room)

You want to know what happened to you, you fucking idiot.

(Stevie remained silent all during what came next and did not reply in any way except to shake his head sheepishly.)

Someone nearly killed you!

For as long as I've known you here at Salve, you've been provoking and injuring innocent people on and off the field.

How many times did you verbally harass the Deaf girl, the Boxman and others?

You never fucking stop.

Did you think you'd never be stopped?

Only an asshole thinks there's no one bigger and badder than themselves. Let me clarify that, only a fucking asshole.

But that's what you thought!

And the rest of us went along with you because we're "team".

But...we're fucking done with that and you! We represent a Christian College. Do you get that?

You fucking hear me?

You want to know what happened looser?

Remember the Deaf girl's friend? Dawn!

Remember her? Ya, that little petite thing.

Remember the times she got in your face and you continued to antagonize her as she tried to protect the Deaf girl, remember that scumbag?

Remember the day she screamed at you, "I swear to God...you'll pay you son of a bitch"? I know you fucking remember that. One thing I know about you is that you have a super keen memory. A god damned genius for all I know. God stuffed an intracranial quantum computer in you, and you chose to weaponize it. You fucking weaponized it!

And another thing, the whole entire campus knows what happened.

What do you remember asshole?

(He wrote on the same piece of paper)

I just remember her crossing the road and nearly getting hit, she was so upset with me.

Well, you goddamn asshole, she made good on her promise! She made real fucking good on her promise!

(In a very low tone of voice) ...so...you want to

know what happened to you?

(Back to screaming) **...that little baby-faced girl came across the street and stood toe to toe with you not saying a word.**

You went to say something and push her away. You tried to push away a girl have your size.

Do you remember that? (Stevie sheepishly shook his head no.)

Well in a split second, she nearly decapitated you. You should be dead! She snapped your jaw clean through, along with major damage to your fucking face. We had to make sure you were breathing. You were, but not properly. EMS had to establish a clear airway. We took turns listening to your breathing until EMS arrived. We all lied about what really happened to EMS and Police.

That little petite thing nearly killed you, how does that sound looser.

There is some tiny little thing you didn't know about her. You would have never known if you weren't a complete prick.

That little girl is a Black Belt in Brazilian Jiu-Jitsu. Let me clarify that! A third-degree Black Belt. How about that, looser.

Only by the grace of God are you still alive.

And one other thing while we're on the subject...

Coach knows what really happened, which

brought a smile to his face. You're off the team, your uniform was confiscated, and your locker emptied.

His exact words were, "Salve's team needs real men, not criminals"

Your Dad had a shit fit.

That little girl didn't kill you, but he might.

Suck that through your fucking straw.

All were still in the cafeteria, the reformed hyenas at their table, the Nursing students at another, and Stevie alone with himself. Glances were continuously made toward Stevie as it became noticeable, he was upset and appeared to be crying, his chest randomly heaving and his hands shaking. He had three separate pieces of paper he was writing on. His condition became more apparent and many began to look in his direction, the volume of conversation dropped precipitously. He rose, returned his tray, and began to walk towards the girls carrying the papers. They could see him coming. Tears were clearly running down his cheeks, but he made no attempt to wipe them. They were dripping off his chin onto the floor. Marcie and Dawn were sitting across from one another, their usual position, so they could see each other signing. They were both at the end of their table and turned themselves toward Stevie when he was just a few feet away. He knelt in front of Dawn first, taking one of her hands in one of his. He held out one of the papers to her other hand. He continued to hold her one hand, his tears now falling on the hands they held. She looked at the note and read it. It said, "Thanks for leaving a little life in me, maybe I can put it to good use? Pray for me." He rose and affectionately kissed her forehead. Next, he kneeled before Marcie holding one of her hands and handing her a note.

He utterly broke down in sobs of tears.

The shame he felt for the verbal insults he had hurled at her... overcame him.

She glanced into his eyes with great pity. Her note said, "Justice came to you, thanks to your dear friend; sorry for everything, my name is Stephen."

He kissed her on the forehead and simultaneously, tenderly touched her cheek.

There was dead silence as he left a trail of tears across the floor and out of the cafeteria.

Next stop was the Boxman. Everything went the same way. When he sat in the plastic folding chair, the Boxman said, "Stephen, I've been praying for you and hoping you'd come". Stephen was noticeably moved. How did he know my name? The Boxman's note read, "Sorry...let me know how I can help". **"Stephen...be good to yourself and others!"** He rose and left, visibly shaken.

Chapter Eight

Sister Mary Mathilda (her professed name), was in deep thought after her visit with the Boxman. She learned he had taken a tiny little apartment close to America's Cup. He told her, he was using the last of his savings and was not from the area. Her great concern was how he was managing to care for himself. His condition was severe. He said, God sent me two angels. I know you know Marcie and Dawn. Each night, one of them meets me at home, feeds me, helps bath me, dress me for sleep and get me in bed. In the morning the other appears to help me get ready and feed me. Who shops for your food? They buy it at Miley. Are you receiving medical care? No.

Several days hence and after deep reflection, Sister called the Dean of Nursing into her office. A long conversation ensued. The two embarked on a plan, something entirely new to the Department of Nursing. The next day a slew of construction vans could be seen at the entrance to Ochre Court. Another important meeting commenced in Sister's office, including the University's architectural firm. Sister knew everyone, as construction and restoration of the College's historic buildings is never ending. The 80-acre campus is one of the most unique in the country, offering what the National Trust for Historic Preservation has described as a "tour of the great architectural works of the Gilded Age." Set on seven contiguous estates, it features more than 20 historic structures that have been sensitively adapted to meet University needs while also preserving their status as treasures of the 19th and early 20th centuries.

The Oceanside setting, however, offers more than a glimpse of the past. Surrounded by rare trees, tide pools and museums, this campus provides access to exceptional learning opportunities for students in many disciplines. Viewed as a "living laboratory", the campus is an extraordinary environment that enriches the City of Newport and contributes to the artistic, cultural, economic, educational and historical vitality of the State of Rhode Island.

This meeting was very different. Sister said to the architects, you will deliver me plans tomorrow morning. Time is not on our side. Everyone walked over to McAuley Hall. Students and staff were somewhat surprised by the procession led by Sister Mathilda down to the basement level. No one, especially staff, was aware of any pending construction. The next morning even more construction crews arrived before daybreak. There was no sign, which would be typical for a new construction project.

Work was furious, multiple dumpsters arrived for demolition materials and construction supplies began arriving at a furious pace all covered by tarps. Work continued around the clock, two shifts, twelve hours each. The lights never turned off and the front entrance doors never locked.

A new concrete ramp to the basement was being erected out back of McAuley (facing the Atlantic Ocean and Cliff Walk), leading from grade level to a new opening at basement level. Two of the four air conditioning compressors that occupied an existing space along that wall had to be relocated. The new ramp would be all poured concrete. It occupied about half of the space already existing along that wall which was topped with a black metal railing.

Sister Matilda and the Dean of Nursing were there multiple times per day. Deliveries of medical equipment could be seen arriving. There was complete "Radio Silence". Only several other people knew; the Board of Trustees and the Chief Financial Officer of the University.

Marcie and Dawn walked by McAuley several times a day, to and fro their dorm room in Reefe Hall. One day, Marcie signed to Dawn, "I wonder what they're doing?" "I have no idea Marcie". On day seven, at the crack of dawn, everything was gone. No construction crews, no dumpsters, no backhoes, no materials, no nothing.

At about 9:00 on the morning of the seventh day, Marcie and Dawn received a text from Sister Matilda, requesting them to report to her office, immediately, and to bring Stephen. Stephen had survived his jaw being wired and could now talk. It was now mid-November.

They arrived, Ochre Court, in the President's Office at 10:00. Only the Dean of Nursing, Sister Matilda and the three. Sister began by saying, Dawn and Marcie; I understand you are both involved with some very important work. Neither spoke. They meekly shook their heads yes. I met with the Boxman and he told me about all the care you are providing him. Well done. I also know this has been a great challenge given his condition. The Nursing Dean had full knowledge of this from Sister. The Dean said, young ladies, this is what we call Palliative Care. It's from the Latin, palliare, meaning "to cloak", as in an outer garment, for protection from the elements! Surely, you've heard of the heavy cloth which drapes a coffin called a pall and the persons who "bear" the coffin called "pallbearers". All part of the same derivation. Medically, it refers to the comfort provided, as relief, from the symptoms, pain and stress of a serious illness. The good Dean, a Doctor of Nursing, had spent significant time in Palliative care at Calvary Hospital in the Bronx, New York.

Calvary Hospital is the nation's only fully accredited acute care specialty hospital devoted to providing palliative care to adults with advanced cancer and other life-limiting illnesses. Since its founding, the hospital's core values have focused on Compassion, respect for the dignity of every patient and non-abandonment of patients and families. Brescia describes the hospital's motivation: "We're different; we're mission driven, Gospel driven. We come across a symptom that is unacceptable, and we treat the symptom until there is relief. Our doctrine is "succor, compassion, love, gentleness". The good Dean was a staunch advocate of Palliative and Hospice care.

I have news for you girls and Stephen. Salve Regina University now has a fully functional Palliative-Hospice Care Center. With Nursing Majors of 60 or so, it will be staffed 24/7/365 on a rotational basis. Three souls will be cared for here.

They all walked down the ramp so as not to draw attention, as the facility had not yet been announced. Their jaws dropped when they entered the basement level. 2,500 square feet with every possible resource imaginable. Stephen, there is a future for you here and you could be very helpful to this mission.

Dawn interpreted for Sister. Marcie, you wrote in your college application essay that you wanted to be a "Compassionate" nurse and the first Deaf Nurse to graduate Salve. You'll accomplish both here...

but especially, in the care of our most vulnerable patients. Sister had no idea of the magnitude of... what she had just said to Marcie!!!

For now, only two persons on earth knew that significance.

Marcie, Dawn and Stephen, bring the Boxman here tonight!

Chapter Nine

One night, Stephen arrived at Dawn and Marcie's dorm room in Reefe Hall. The door was open. There were several girls in the room but not Marcie; she was at her private dance lesson. He knocked and said, I'd like to speak to Dawn in private. There was a little apprehension on Dawn's part as she would be all alone with the person she nearly killed.

He sat down on one of the beds and was scanning the room. He saw numerous pictures of Dawn and Marcie together in high school but what really jumped out at him were pictures of Dawn during martial arts competitions. Stephen did not say anything for a minute or so. Dawn stayed standing. One of the girls stood just outside the open door.

Please tell me about yourself and Marcie. That one question took her thirty minutes to answer. He was hoping to hear something about Marcie's dancing but did not. He had heard about Marcie and her dancing but previously cared less. Since he had such a keen memory, he clearly remembers someone describing her as a world class dancer. Can you tell me something about her dance? Another ten minutes passed. How can she dance if she can't hear? Stephen, I'm going to have you find out. Do a little research and go watch her. Where? Antone Academic Center. But where in the Center? Follow the music. He hugged Dawn closely and placed his poor cheek against hers and said thanks.

Once outside he immediately sat on a bench with his smart phone. In no time, he was dumbfounded to learn about the Departments of Theatre, Music and Dance. He clicked on "Images" and was blown away. During his entire life he had absolutely no exposure to the Arts. His entire life had been football. He was totally unprepared by what he found upon entering the Antone Center.

Just as Dawn had said, he could clearly hear loud music down the hall and followed the sound. She was in the Winn Dance Studio (scroll through previous link). He looked in and observed Marcie in a symphony of movement. It enthralled him. Marcie danced with her eyes closed moving with magical grace in ways Stephen did not know possible. Katherine was off to the side. He entered while Marcie was still dancing in her trance like state. She had no awareness of him. He saw some plastic folding chairs along one wall and immediately saw Sister Mathilda sitting there. Since the music was deafening, Sister motioned to him and pointed to the seat next to her. The Dance continued for another seven minutes or so. He surely knew both songs. Marcie, eyes still closed, swirled in a magical universe, which could take your breath away. Stephen had never witnessed the energy being expended not even on a football field. He couldn't get past the sheer power of what he was seeing. Those who witnessed Marcie dance were left speechless. As no words could describe it. The word, if there was one was, ...WOW!

Her dance ended in a climax of sheer physical endurance. She was completely spent. When Marcie saw Stephen, she was surprised but waved to him and walked over to Katherine. Stephen returned the next night, with a pen and notepad. He scribbled notes on the pad feverishly. No one asked him why. And then he disappeared. He never asked Sister why she was there nor vice versa.

One small detail about Stephen, that his former hyena roommate screamed at him, was that Stephen had a keen memory. Probably genetic or a complication of the football "Game Film" his Dad had him watching at three years old. Same, in a general sense to "NFL Coaches Film" used for game analysis. Coaches Film is comprised of two main camera angles: "All-22" and "High End Zone." The "All 22" camera is positioned high above the NFL playing field and shows a view of the field that includes all 22 players (11 on offense, 11 on defense) at the same time. This All-22 camera view can be used to analyze all plays and players on any given play in an NFL game. Whatever it took to produce a "Winner". What no one knew was, Stephen arrived early the second night and concealed a motion activated camera he was streaming to his laptop. Mission complete! For the next two days, no one saw Stephen, even at classes, except in a small room, number 306, located in McKillop Library. It had a large glass window facing the interior of the third floor and another overlooking the stairwell. He looked so intense, no one ever went in. He stared at the laptop for hours on end. Steven was a savant of sorts, either by genetics or his Father's training. What Stephen could pick out from Game Film was beyond what any coach was seeing. Not only could he pick out such minutia, it instantly streamed to his "Human Hard Drive" for immediate recall later. This was what made him a great football player, except, by virtue of his "Nature", a dangerous one as well.

The tale of two plans! No one had any idea what Stephen was up to, at least not yet. However, there was a secret plan between Sister, Katherine and Marcie. It was thought of by Sister. The plan was, that Marcie would dance for all to see, and to showcase the Dance program at the Governor's Ball, held the first Saturday in December. This grand Ball started over forty years ago when, the Governor of the State of Rhode Island was asked to be the Guest of Honor at a fundraising event for scholarships. Every sitting Governor has honored the invitation since. It is a black-tie event, currently exceeding 600 guests, which takes place in the Grand Ochre Court Mansion donated by Mr.& Mrs. Goulet. It is an event like no other. It encompasses all the levels of the Mansion. It currently raises about a half million dollars. Stephen didn't know about this plan, at least not yet. Stephen had his own plan.

Chapter Ten

On the evening of the seventh day, when the Palliative-Hospice Center was completed, Stephen said to the two girls, I'll go get him tonight. By yourself? Yes. I need to talk to him. 8:00 right? Yes.

Promptly at 8:00 Stephen arrived at America's Cup. He had a very funny feeling when he arrived at the spot where his life was nearly snuffed out. The Boxman was already told to expect Stephen. Hello Stephen, good to see you. Now, it's a good walk from Americas Cup to Ochre Point Avenue and McAuley Hall especially when pushing a wheelchair, but that had no effect on Stephen, a perfect human specimen. They talked all the way there. Or should we say, Stephen talked all the way there. When they passed the turn where the Boxman had been living, he said to Stephen, you're going the wrong way. Stephen said, we are going somewhere special. The Boxman thought he might be taking him to some restaurant. It wasn't till they passed Miley Hall that the Boxman, who was very familiar with the Salve Campus, asked Stephen again, "where are we going". Miley would have been the last place to eat before the Atlantic Ocean. Stephen said, just two blocks more, passing Ochre Court along the way. The Boxman really had no idea except that perhaps they were headed to Reefe Hall to visit Dawn and Marcie. But suddenly, Michael turned left at McAuley Hall and said...you're home! What do you mean, I'm home? You'll see! They rounded the left side of the building and the Boxman could see this ramp. Stephen, where are we going? Home!

The ramp was beautifully illuminated with bright LED lighting. At the bottom he saw a door with a handicapped push button. Stephen said...go ahead, push it! Stephen wheeled him through and there were Marcie, Dawn, the Dean and Sister all holding Mylar balloons. On cue they all said, "Welcome Home". The Boxman, a man of few words, was silent. He was looking all around, at what could not possibly be true, tears running down his cheeks.

Marcie knelt, held his frail hands in hers, and with both their tears, falling on both their hands;

she "verbally" said... "you're home"!

The Boxman understood her clearly!

There were Nursing students in their scrubs off to the side. They would be taking care of the Boxman tonight, doing all the things that Marcie and Dawn had been doing and then some. They had already received intense training as did every other nursing student and they knew what to do. The girls were ready to leave when Marcie ran her fingers through what was left of the Boxman's hair saying aloud, **have a good night.** Again, he understood her voice clearly. As they neared the door, the Boxman said in a very frail voice, where is Stephen? Right behind you. Stephen come here. Stephen knelt. The Boxman leaned close and whispered something into his ear. The three left and were all on cloud nine. As Reefe hall was literally just yards away, Stephen, walked between both girls holding each of their hands. Nothing was said, there were no words for that. At Reefe, he affectionately kissed both on the head and headed off to his own dorm room in the Young Building on Bellevue, also home to the Pell Honors Program. Perhaps, nowhere else, would your "Dorm" room be in a stately 1850's Queen Anne-Style Mansion on the famous Bellevue Avenue in Newport.

Since the Boxman hadn't received any medical care for several months already, the nurses did a complete assessment and he answered as many questions as his stamina could allow. When, he sensed they were finished he said to the three students, girls, come here. Please don't trouble yourselves with so much paperwork. Surely you all know I'm dying. Just do the best you can, to help me cross the "Threshold of Hope".

Chapter Eleven

Oh, Stephen... where in the world are you? Stephen had gone, "Radio Silent", for two days now but was about to reappear. It was about 9:30 P.M. when he left his dorm in the Young building headed to the Antone Center, named after the good Sister Antone a former President of Salve. He knew Marcie's private lessons ended at 10:00 P.M. He positioned himself under the huge Beech Tree behind McKillop Library with a good view of the Antone Academic Center and the door that he knew Marcie would exit. It was totally dark so no one would see him, especially Campus Security. Like clockwork, Marcie walked out alone at 10:05. He waited till she was far enough away as not to see him. He was not there to see Marcie. In he went and down the hallway to Winn Dance Studio where he knew Katherine would be. Of course, he did not address her as Katherine but as Professor. She turned to see Stephen at the door of the studio. She knew his name, as she had asked Sister who he was the first night he appeared to watch Marcie. Katharine had heard the now infamous story about Stephen, but she had no idea this was "that" Stephen. Do you have a few minutes, I know it's late? Sure, I do. What's up?

I wanted to ask you something. Stephen had no idea about the plan for the Governor's Ball. He said... would you teach me the dance that Marcie is doing? I don't understand. I'd like to someday be her dance partner if I had someone to teach me. Stephen, you do not know what you are asking. It's taken Marcie her whole life to become the dancer she is, coupled with the fact she has God given talent that I have not witnessed before. Have you ever danced? Only on the football field. A light bulb lit in Katherine's brain. Are you that Stephen? Unfortunately, the answer to that question would be yes. I was aware through Dawn and Marcie of the serious issues they had with you and I am fully aware of the outcome. So, why do you want to dance with Marcie? I just do.

I have no other way to explain it to you. How could you possibly learn this with such short notice? What do you mean, short notice? Stephen, have a seat. I'm going to share something with you that only a handful of people know about. If word of what I'm going to share with you ever leaves your lips, that would be disastrous. When Sister Mathilda and I became aware of the extreme dance talent that Marcie has, Sister Mathilda, decided she'd ask her to do a solo dance at the Governor's Ball. That's only about a month and a half away. It is not possible that even a seasoned dancer could rise to her level in anywhere close to that amount of time. That's just impossible! How can you imagine that could be possible?

I can imagine how, but it would be difficult to explain. Well, go ahead and try. All my life I've been viewing football game tapes. Stephen what is a game tape? He explained. I have some unique capability to see detail that no one else sees and I guess I do have a photographic memory, at least that's what people tell me. I can absorb massive amounts of data and sort of digitize it in my brain. Recall, of whatever I just saw, is crystal clear, like I'm watching a game tape. That's very interesting Stephen, as I see the same thing with Marcie. Keep going. So, I taped her dance. What do you mean? I set up a secret camera the second night I was here and taped it. You know Stephen that could get someone in serious trouble. What do I have to lose? I'm already thought of as a pariah on this campus. I've disgraced my family and this University. I have nothing left to lose and nearly lost life itself. I did it because I want to dance with her. O.K. Stephen, I'll pretend I never heard that. For days now, I've been holed up in McKillop running her dance through the same database in my brain that I use to break down game tapes. I have every fucking, (excuse me), step already cataloged in my brain. In my brain...subatomic particles exist in more than one state at any one time! O.K. Stephen, except I have no idea what you just said!

Stephen based upon what you tell me, it might be a one in a million chance that I could teach you her dance. But there is something I do not believe you can understand. Marcie is deaf as you well know. You made it your "pastime" to taunt her over that. Marcie is different. She draws her talent from a reservoir of energy that is both genetic and spiritual. Marcie has extremely limited sound recognition even with the volume you have personally experienced. Her body has adapted to this limitation in ways that science does not completely understand. All her other senses conspire with each other to make accommodations for her loss of hearing. Truth be told, it's as if her DNA can think! Do you understand what I am saying to you? She dances in another dimension. Stephen, can you feel music? No. Well Marcie can! I can't teach you that. Would you give it a try? O.K. But prepare yourself for failure. Marcie is not to know anything about this. Meet me right here at 7:00 A.M.

Stephen, I've been up half the night. Do you realize I spent my life earning a PhD in Dance and I truthfully do not know how to proceed? By the way, call me Katherine. I've thought of only one approach that I believe has any chance of success. Listen to me very carefully. You can't understand Marcie's world and especially her dance world because you have all your senses. Do you understand that? Yes. The only way you could possibly enter her world is to live in her world. I am loaning you some things from the Department of Music and Theatre. You will use them to enter her world. You will not shower for the next 48 hours and you will never, not for a single second, remove them until I see you two days from now in this same room. If you fail this test, it's over. You will not speak to anyone, you will not ask anyone for help, unless you get hit by a car. Do you agree? Yes.

Come over here. Since this is a "crash" course we must speed things up. We're going to take away three of your senses for the next two days. Two will be of the five basic senses and the third will be a lesser known sense. Place these ear plugs in your ears and then place these ear protectors over that. He did. She said something to him, and he did not hear her. One sense gone. She handed him a cane with some red tape wrapped around its bottom tip. Next, she placed a very tight-fitting black mask over his eyes. She made a quick gesture as if she was going to punch him in the face. He did not flinch. Two senses gone. Finally, she carefully, as she could see he was not completely healed, placed a piece of duct tape over his mouth. She realized he should acclimate well to the loss of speech since his jaws had been wired shut for weeks.

She walked away and never looked back.

OMG, he didn't make it out of Antone Center before smashing his face on the door jamb. That face was not accustomed to such trauma since his little encounter with Dawn. It took him a half hour to make it back to his dorm room. He was in a new universe and probably not a parallel one. He was no longer in the universe he'd been since birth. He had no idea, but traffic came to a standstill each time he crossed a road, people could not believe what they were seeing. Everywhere he went or tried to go, was fraught with intense trepidation. It almost seemed cruel to witness. Anyone who knew Stephen, pretty much everyone, all realized who it was. People didn't know whether to laugh or cry. His first matter of business was to go to Miley Hall cafeteria as he realized he was quite hungry especially since he had lost significant weight drinking liquids for so long. To his great testament, he was 100% determined and never felt self-pity. He was drawing upon his football experience to pull through. Had he known what was coming he could have prepared. With his keen mind he could have counted and easily remembered the number of steps to each building and between each block, but this was cold turkey. Groups of people stopped dead in their tracks to witness this amazing sight. He nearly fell off every curb and tripped over the next. As he approached Miley, with hordes of students approaching as well, something happened causing a gasp by all onlookers. As he approached the stairs of Miley, he didn't know where they were. He hit the first of the four exterior stairs and fell forward and couldn't get his hands out in time. He smashed his face into the fourth step. Yes, in the same exact spot as Dawn's footprint. He just lay there. The pain was so intense he was crying. Several students went to help him but when he felt their hands, he pushed them away. His arms were straight out as a signal that he did not want help.

He wanted to dance with Marcie, and this was the price of admission. His face immediately swelled up. He steadied himself and made it to the interior doors of the cafeteria. Not that he could hear anything anyways, but there was dead silence. No matter what anyone was doing, they stopped dead in their tracks. All the cafeteria employees knew him because of his special dietary needs for weeks. He stumbled up to what he perceived was one of several serving stations. He had obtained a pad of paper and a pen from his dorm room and wrote what he wanted on a piece of paper, holding it out and hoping someone would take it. They did. He was confused as to how he would find a table and chair. Holding his tray with one hand and the cane in the other it was as if the Red Sea had parted as students hastily got out of his way. He carefully peeled back the duct tape just enough to get food in his mouth. He thought… Katherine would not have denied me nourishment? Katherine had called Sister Mathilda, 5:00 that morning, to relay her plan. Sister texted Marcie and Dawn saying, text me when Stephen arrives at Miley. They had no idea why. Now they knew. Sister arrived minutes later. When she entered, everyone took notice. Stephen could not hear nor see as she addressed the entire cafeteria. Students, I trust you have all heard the Biblical story of Saul being knocked off his horse. Stephen has chosen a similar trial to serve a greater purpose. You all know Stephen and his recent trials and tribulations.

Saul and following his conversion, Paul, became a missionary and wrote one quarter of the New Testament. What you are witnessing today are the Gospels coming alive in this very place. If you have eyes that see and ears that hear, realize the great teaching moment that God has placed before you. Stephen has chosen this path towards his own conversion. Pray for him. Sister walked over to Marcie and Dawn telling them, take the Boxman to and fro his "Spot" for the next two days. Then she left.

What Stephen could not possibly have known is that Sister already had met with Security early that morning after Katherine's call. From the moment he exited Antone Center he was being followed both by foot and car with flashing lights. Every intersection he came upon, the security vehicle took position in the intersection. Someone was always twenty or so feet behind him. They followed him into the Young building each time he entered until they saw him enter his room. A security vehicle with strobe lights flashing, round the clock, stood vigil outside Young unless Stephen was on the move. Everyone knew why.

There was little conversation as Stephen was in Miley. This was an event that affected everyone in a profound way. Mostly, they watched Stephen. When it was time for him to leave, eyes were riveted upon him as he fumbled to return his tray down a short hallway with a sign hanging from the ceiling reading "Dish Return". Again, he banged into the half wall where the conveyor belt for trays is located, but was successful, nonetheless. Security blocked Ochre Point Avenue as it became clear he was headed towards Ochre Court. It was just a little easier for him, as he remembered that there were three portals to that Main gate the center one with a sign reading Salve Regina University. He remembered that the smaller gates to each side, led to gravel stone walkways. The large center gate had a paved driveway. All three led to the entrance. He reasoned that he would stay on one of the smaller gravel pathways since any deviation would mean he was on the grass and off the path. He somehow found the huge glass door making sure he did not trip again on any stair. One-by-one he made it up the Grand Staircase to the second floor. The Goulet's gift of Ochre Court to the Sisters of Mercy would be in excess of one hundred million dollars today. Stephen had some recollection of where the President's Office was as he'd been there before. Once to be threatened with expulsion and the last time with Marcie and Dawn. But his memory wasn't crystal clear, so he first wandered into the room that was originally the Nursery. Eventually, he made it to Sister's office with Security watching his every step. He felt her hand on his shoulder which he did not push away. She helped him into a chair. He wrote on his pad of paper. Sister, I am changing my Major to Education. I will not begin till next semester. I have some things to take care of which will require all my time. He held out the note. Sister read it and tapped him on the shoulder twice which he interpreted as O.K.? Security walked backwards down the grand stairway just three feet ahead of him in case he was to trip. He made it.

One of his former football friends, videoed him walking to Ochre Court and sent it to Stephen's Father with absolutely no audio.

Since he was now done with classes till next semester he headed back to Young. Marcie and Dawn were following behind. Marcie could not have known that Stephen was amassing the necessary funds to dance with her. The girls had an idea, even though they had seen his reaction to people trying to help him when he smashed his face at Miley. They would each approach him, one on each side and simultaneously take one hand. Stephen just knew it was them and did not push them away. He did not know, which was which, but tears dripped beneath his eye mask. Stephen had a great awakening as he thought, so...this is "Compassion". They walked him to the Cliff Walk behind the Breakers Mansion. The walkway splits into two separate levels. In between, is a granite wall with a metal railing which separates the two levels. In the middle of the lower level is a granite bench which they guided him to. He sat down. The granite wall adjacent to the lower sidewalk, facing the Atlantic and the precipice below, would shortly play an important role. He had already figured he was on the Cliff walk, just based upon the general direction they were leading him. He was now replaying his "Game Tapes" of Campus in his mind. He could also feel the wind and saltwater spray which helped dry his cheeks. They kissed his face, one on each side, placed their hands, one on top of each other on his head, and held them there for some time in prayer. Then they left him to be with his own thoughts.

Chapter Twelve

Not more than five minutes after Stephen left Sister's office, her secretary alerted her that Stephen's father was on the phone. Sister, someone just sent me a video of Stephen. What in God's name is going on? Dad had barely had enough time to digest the fact that Stephen had been thrown off the team. Mr. Burns, Stephen has decided to make some changes in his life. Those changes have already had a profound effect on himself and this University. Trust that Stephen has embarked on a road less travelled and his journey is already bearing good fruit. I am aware of all that is happening and am monitoring the situation very closely. Trust in me and Stephen that you will find great joy in the decisions Stephen is making. I just had a visit from Stephen. He shared with me that he is changing majors and will be very busy and not attending classes the duration of this semester. Mr.

Burns, as you know, the University is enormously thankful for the financial gift you have made to fund the new "Center". We trust that you have full faith and confidence in us! The gifts Stephen is bestowing upon us cannot be measured in financial terms and for this we are most grateful. Please, trust in our Lord, in all these things.

Mr. Burns, I know you are a man of great wealth. Your son presented me with a note several minutes ago which contained the information I just relayed to you. However, there was another part of his message to me. Two requests. It said, if my Dad calls…ask him to transfer to my personal bank account, $250,000. If he asks why, just tell him I need it. The second message for you was, "make sure you and Mom are at the Governor's Ball". Mr. Burns, that's all I know at the present time. Please tell Stephen, the funds will be in his account in 48 hours. Mr. Burns, God has chosen Stephen for a purpose that only He knows. Trust in that. I'll update you as necessary.

The Boxman was increasingly ill. His hands and head shook without ceasing and he could no longer feed himself, even with "weighted" utensils. Also, his cancer symptoms accelerated, and his appearance changed dramatically. However, he arrived as always, at his home away from home. Now people were lined up before his arrival. He would not disappoint them. He would be properly clothed by his nurses and wrapped in warm blankets. Someone had run a very long extension cord to the closest building and plugged in a heating pad for his lap. He never, ever complained. A local restaurant was now setting up a table each day with coffee and pastries, as it was growing colder, and people were waiting for long periods. Marcie and Dawn were frequent visitors. They and others were closely tending to all his needs. They had eyes which could see, and as nursing students themselves, they realized the Boxman was on borrowed time. It was now common to see all three, Marcie, Dawn and Stephen, all together at night bringing him home to McAuley. Little was said during these journeys.

As always, everyone who entered to speak with the Boxman received his brief and compassionate message to them and his shaking hand extended to momentarily lie on their head.

Stephen had made huge inroads into the world of the blind and deaf and by the second day of his trial had defied all the odds. He was now walking at a brisk pace having made "Game Tapes" of all his journeys. It appeared he had all his "Counting" done, seemingly having "sight". Stepping down curbs and up the next. All were fascinated. At times he could be seen swirling his cane.

And so, on the end of the second day, he arrived in Katherine's studio in Antone Center as directed. He was sitting there when she entered. She had also been closely monitoring this situation with

Sister. It was 7:00 A.M. when she placed her hand on his shoulder, so he'd know she was there. He didn't know but Sister, Marcie, and, Dawn were beside him. Sister had already alerted Security to call off the surveillance. Katherine carefully removed his mouth tape and eye mask. His eyes opened brightly, and he saw them all. He removed his hearing protectors and ear plugs. You could see his senses were in overload after their sensory deprivation. He didn't speak, as his senses had not kicked in yet. He just sat there looking around.

Katherine spoke first, Stephen, you have passed your test. Remember my promise? Stephen, when I was in College one of my Professor's had a sign on her classroom door. It read..."It is kind of fun to do the impossible". You and I are going to have fun doing the impossible. Be back here after you shower and eat. Boost your caloric intake as you'll need it. Be back here ASAP.

And, oh Ya, bring your "Game Tape". Marcie and Dawn had no clue what she was talking about. Sister did.

Stephen's football friends saw him come into Miley. They sat with him. His roommate, the one who launched into a ballistic tirade when Stephen asked him "what happened", said to him...Coach has seen you these past two days and knows all that has happened. With Sister's blessing he took a vote of the entire team whether we'd agree or not to reinstate you. All voted yes. When I see Coach,

I'll thank him and Sister, but I have things I need to do. Thank you all, but I need to decline.

When Stephen returned to Katharine, she said to him. Stephen... now we have something to work with. Show me your "Game Tape", and he opened his laptop. Stephen, what do you see? Katherine, when I watch this, I see something I've not seen before. Such as? I didn't know the human body could do things like this. Stephen, that's because it's the human mind that's doing these things. Marcie's mind feels these things and her mind produces the movement. This is different! Tell me what your "Game Tape" reveals to you? It's complex, very complex. I break all the sequences down in my brain into smaller fragments. Each sequence a small "Game Tape". I have immediate recall. So then Stephen, we need to start by breaking down the steps and movements. Let's start with the "Steps". Get out on the floor and without any music, do as many of the steps as you can. Katharine was amazed. It was rough, but all the basic steps were there. Stephen, I have several classes. I want you to do these steps, over and over and over till you're exhausted. Marcie, as you know, takes her dance to the point of ultimate exhaustion because she's using her mind to overcome her disability and, in a very real sense, over-achieving. Feeling sound, takes incredibly more mental energy than hearing sound. Just like lip reading, it is mentally exhausting. I'll return in about three hours. Don't stop. The only way you can stop is to collapse. And so, he did, over and over and over till she returned. All Katherine could think about during her classes is how Stephen could be capable of the things he was. She began to focus her mind on the similarities between dance and football. She began to realize in her mind, that each play in football was a short dance. She was making her own "Game Tape". Every time the ball is snapped, twenty-two players execute a short dance. Some, tete-a-tete, others intimate in nature, as defensive players cover pass receivers but can't interfere with their partner. Some incredibly evasive, as running backs twist and weave away from defensive players, all in all, an intricate dance. She dwelled on this hypothesis a lot.

When she returned, Stephen was still dancing, and yeah, exhausted. She said, Stephen, I know you have always been a supreme athlete. I would imagine you have spent your lifetime in gyms, building up your stamina. However, as important as that has been, you'll need more. Presently, you will not keep up with Marcie. You need long distance endurance training. For the rest of today, you will run and run and run till you can't run any more. See how many times you can run Cliff Walk, back and forth.

And each time you come upon the Forty Steps, run up and down them as well. Just do it till you freaking collapse. That's the only way you'll be able to keep up with her. And take earphones and listen to the music. Do not stop till you collapse. You will do this every single day.

Later that evening, when he was completely spent, he was walking back to Young. He entered Keefe Hall and went to Dawn and Marcie's room. The door was open, and he could see both at their desks studying. Dawn interpreted to Marcie that "he needs to speak to me". Since Marcie couldn't hear anyways, she continued to study. Stephen said to Dawn, I need you to teach me as much "Sign" in four weeks as is humanly possible. O.K? May I ask what for? I can't tell you now. Where can we meet each night, so Marcie doesn't know? Room 306 in Mckillop Library. Can we begin right now? See you there in ten minutes. And so, just like four years prior, when Dawn became Marcie's student, the gift would be paid forward. They were there till 2:00 A.M. Now both were spent. Stephen's quest was firing on all cylinders. Mornings dancing, watching "Game Tapes", not only of Marcie but of himself, running, learning American Sign Language and a lot more that no one even knew about except Sister and the co-chairs of the Governor's Ball. Stephen had the funds he had requested from his Dad. During every available moment, he had communications concerning his "Plan", halfway around the world.

Chapter Thirteen

About a week had passed and Marcie signed to Dawn, where has Stephen been? I don't know Marcie. I hear he's been very busy. Word began to spread that quite a few students were watching him dance with Katherine. Students, who were minoring in Dance and others from Dance SRU, frequently would be seen at the studio door. Some came in and watched. No one minded. Since it was not something Marcie knew either, she had no idea until she stayed behind after one of her "Private" lessons and saw Stephen enter Antone Center. Her curiosity was peaked especially since she hadn't seen him in a week. Katherine and Stephen were studying the "Game Tape" as Marcie walked in. She could see him in Dance attire. She didn't understand. They continued looking at the "laptop" until Marcie took her cue and left. From here on in, that door would remain closed. Marcie also asked Dawn where she went each night and why she came back so late. All she said was, Sister assigned me a special project, helping another "Student". Marcie assumed she meant a "Nursing" student and dropped the subject. Only one day, Marcie was in McKillop to study and just so happened to go to the third floor. There she saw Stephen, all alone, with his laptop in the "little" room, hands flying a mile a minute. Mile a minute or not she could read the sign. It wasn't great but readable. Over and over he signed the exact same thing.

"Marcie can I have this" ...

"Marcie can I have this" ... *"Marcie can I have this".*

At least ten times, as she stood where he would not see her. Total confusion. Marcie immediately texted Dawn saying, "Do you have any idea why Stephen is "Signing" here at McKillop? What do you mean? I'm watching him in room 306 signing the same thing repeatedly. What's he signing? "Marcie, can I have this"... repeatedly! Marcie, meet me at Our Lady of Mercy Chapel in fifteen minutes.

Dawn arrived first and was sitting in one of the pews. Marcie was very concise. Dawn, what's going on? Marcie, remember when you asked me why I came back to our room so late. I told you I was helping a student. Well, that's true. What I didn't tell you was, the student was Stephen. What do you mean? Remember the night he came over and said he needed to speak to me. That's when he asked me to teach him ASL. He wouldn't tell me why. All he said was, "I want to ask Marcie something", in "her" language. That's all I know. And, why do I see him at the Antone Center? When we were all there the day he removed his blindfold, etc., no one knew why he had done that and neither did Katharine or Sister tell us anything. Marcie, that I do not know. Why not text Stephen and ask him? I just might. I'll do it later, thanks Dawn.

Text from Sister to Marcie, Dawn and Stephen. "Go get the Boxman. He's not well. Please confirm." Got it. Got it. Got it. They all arrived, after running the whole way. The Boxman was having trouble speaking. Dawn signed to Marcie; I think it's a stroke. Marcie signed back. No, it's his tumor. Tumor? Yes, brain tumor. How do you know, what tumor? I know from the "Center", he has a brain tumor. O.K. Let's call an ambulance. No! No! He doesn't want that. Marcie, how do you know that?

Marcie moved by emotion yelled, "I know!".

Dawn understood her clearly. Let's get him back home. Stephen raced him back as the girls ran beside. That evening, after all the nursing students' great care, he asked all three to come into his room separately. Stephen was first, then Dawn and lastly Marcie. When it was Marcie's turn, Dawn signed to her, won't you need me to interpret? No, I'll be O.K. They could hear Marcie speaking in there but could not make anything out. The Boxman understood clearly. He was a keen listener. Each was in there about five minutes. Sister was in the hallway with them. Each heard something special from the Boxman, as his speech was back to normal, followed by a hug and the gentle touch on their head.

When Marcie left the Boxman's room, Stephen turned to Sister and said. The plan! Time is of the essence! 8:00 A.M. tomorrow. Ochre. This was all signed to Marcie. Neither girl understood. The three walked hand in hand until they arrived at Reefe and Stephen continued on.

7:45 A.M. Ochre. Every vehicle from Security arrived on Webster Street alongside Ochre Court with several Newport Police as well. Everyone in Miley, including the girls, could see all the flashing lights and everyone exited Miley and walked in the direction of Ochre, just across the street. Police and security let all enter Webster alongside the great lawn behind Ochre Court. No one had any idea what was going on. Police and security formed a perimeter around Ochre Court. Sister knew why...the "Plan".

Everyone seemed perplexed by the perimeter, as no one could be seen entering or exiting Ochre Court.

Suddenly, you heard this roar and people started to point at the Ocean. Marcie couldn't hear anything but could see what everyone was pointing at. The closer it got, the louder the roar. It came in at an unusually steep angle of descent as if it were in a hurry. The rotor wash was incredible. Everyone's hair was unrecognizable. Police and Security had to remove their hats. When it landed everyone could see Sikorsky S-76C on its side.

After thirty seconds or so, Stephen could be seen exiting Ochre Court and crossing the lawn carrying a briefcase. The Great Lawn behind Ochre Court is two separate levels with a short stone wall separating them. The S-76-C was on the upper level close to the building. He glanced at the crowd and immediately spotted Dawn and Marcie. He stopped and slowly walked under the rotor wash without the slightest concern. He stopped as the crowd looked on. He signed to them both. "I have something to take care of".

He kissed both under the rotor wash

and returned to the open door.

Everyone recognized Stephen. He entered the open door, it closed, and the rotor began to whirl at an enormous speed. It took off as suddenly as it arrived with a steep angle of ascent. It banked steeply over the ocean, destination Logan. All anyone could say was, Wow!

8:30 A.M., EST. Four corporate jets take off from two different time zones around the globe. Two from Logan, one from New York City and one from London. Destination? Reykjavik, Iceland. Stephen's would be the first to land.

Stephen's plan was unfolding as the result of intense planning. He was flush with cash, thanks to his Dad. Stephen was an avid fan of all thing's music. The first night he watched Marcie dancing he immediately realized something about the two songs she had chosen. It is highly unlikely that Marcie realized that both lead singers had collaborated to produce Princess of China on the Mylo Xyloto album in early 2012, and a video featuring both singers. Very few people would have remembered that. Stephen's love of music and his photographic memory did not fail him. From the moment he became aware of the "Dance" that Marcie would perform at the Governor's Ball he imagined both bands, and a third, performing live for Marcie. This wasn't part of the price of admission but a gift he hoped to give her. He also hoped he would be dancing with her, but she could potentially say no. He had a plan for when he would say, "Marcie can I have this..." One thing he knew was that Marcie was extremely fond of the music she had chosen. Not just for the big sound but she loved both lead singers and their bands. Not in a million years would she have imagined a gift like this. She was a diminutive Deaf girl. Unpretentious.

Upon Stephen's arrival, he checked into the Hilton Reykjavik Nordica about 3.8 km from the airport. It was not lost on Stephen that on October 11-12, 1986 the summit between Mikhail Gorbachev and Ronald Reagan took place here resulting in the 1987 Intermediate Range Nuclear Forces Treaty. He imagined this as his very own high stakes summit. If this place could host a Superpower nuclear treaty summit, why not his "Superpower Plan"? Stephen had arranged all the necessary lodging and conference rooms for the three bands and their entourage, including the "animals". Rihanna from New York was the second to land and arrive at the hotel. Next came Coldplay from London and finally Brass Attack from Cumberland, Rhode Island. Brass Attack is a nine-piece band featuring four horns, a rhythm section, and five lead vocalists - one female and four male - performing classic hits from the 1930's up to today! They've been together for over thirty years and played for Presidents George H.W. Bush and William J. Clinton. They've been playing the Governor's Ball for as long as anyone remembers. Stephen greeted all upon arrival, thirty or so. He was deeply involved with Hilton staff as several large box trucks arrived with instruments, speakers, luggage, etc.

Later that afternoon, when all equipment was assembled, they all met in the appointed conference room. It was a happy reunion between Rihanna, Chris Martin and their bands. All from Brass Attack were warmly welcomed into the fold. Stephen had intense interactions with all three bands for about a month now. It was time for all to watch, the "Secret Game Tape", which he had recorded the second night he watched Marcie dancing at Antone Center. He streamed it to a very large screen in that conference room. Took Stephen about 30 minutes to break it down in fine detail. In the course of the review someone said, Stephen you are right, no one dances like that! She's Deaf?

The "Summit" was necessary to plan out the entire sequence of the music and a myriad of details, including the volume of the sound. He came with a decibel meter. Stephen's planning for Game Day had been intense beyond belief. He had his own drone which he expertly flew for years now. He videoed a sequence of the drone approaching Salve from over the ocean with its first view of the Breakers Mansion directly across from Marcie and Dawn's dorm in Reefe Hall. Reefe came into view as it passed over and you could plainly see all the detail of Ochre Court Avenue with images of McAuley, McKillop, and Miley. As it turned, it made a complete pass around Ochre Court including the Great Lawn and the wrought iron gate with the sign reading "Salve Regina University". They were all surprised by the next sequence. Someone is standing at the two very large front glass doors of Ochre Court and the drone flies directly inside. Stephen shot detailed images of the Main Hall, the Grand Staircase, the balconies and finally paused in front of a plaque titled "Gratitude". As it flies out the doors again, the image ends. Someone said, wow Stephen, you've left no stone unturned. One of the members of Brass Attack asked Stephen to stop the video at one point so they could explain to everyone where they set up each year in front of one of the fireplaces large enough to walk into. This was key information as all equipment for all three bands would have to be located there as well. Stephen had already contracted with a local Newport electrical firm to carefully oversee all the electrical needs necessary to power this operation, evaluating "draw", checking breakers, etc., and final setup for the Ball. This firm was already in touch with the technical geniuses of the three bands. The sequence of the entire event was carefully laid out by Stephen.

For the next hour or so, he laid out the "Game Tape" for them that he had intimately created in his mind. Where and when Marcie would enter the Main Hall? What she would be wearing? Where the football team would be? Where members of Sigma Phi Sigma would be? They are the "National Mercy Honor Society" which among other things, represent the University at Convocation and the Governor's Ball. Where would the drone be? Where would Katherine and Sister Mathilda be? Where would the Governor be? Where would the "Animals" be? And, Dawn? Where would he be? Where would staff and friends from ASD be? And the detail which worried him most...where, (God willing) would the Boxman be?

He covered each detail in explicable detail. All looked on in amazement. What is your major, Stephen? He didn't answer except to say, "It's not about me".

Stephen had unique talents. He wasn't watching football game tapes anymore, but he was a fervent consumer of music videos. He was also fascinated by the space program, in particular, the Space-X program. He was enamored with the launch of the Space X Falcon Heavy Lift Rocket. He watched the

YouTube video countless times. Stephen equated this present challenge to "Lift-Off". The details of the plan, now unfolding, had a parallel relationship to Falcon Heavy. Securely in his mind, was "Lift-Off.

In Stephen's mind, he was currently at T minus five seconds. At T minus one minute, computers had already taken control of the countdown. T minus thirty, the water cannons had already opened.

T minus twenty, Falcon go for launch, T minus fifteen, Falcon Heavy was configured for flight. He was now at T minus five seconds, as water cannons open full bore sending millions of gallons of water onto the launch pad.

He was now fully engrossed with "Lift-Off". He would not quit, he would not rest, until the side boosters had initiated their landing burns, the side booster landing legs had deployed, and the Falcons had landed. That's how he saw it.

He continuously prayed for the Boxman.

Stephen had the full choreography in his mind and continued to spew details, like an erupting volcano. It was silent in the room. He explained how he had watched the "Official" videos of Rihanna's, "We found Love" and Coldplay's, "A Sky Full of Stars", the songs Marcie had chosen. He knew every step of the dance. He explained how the choreography would be the main detail now. How Brass Attack would meld with the other bands, Where Marcie would be, hopefully with him, as the music began. Where and when, Coldplay would begin, "A sky full of Stars", well before entering Ochre Court. The illumination of Ochre Point Avenue from Reefe to Ochre and on tops of which buildings those spotlights would be. Police and security and how the entire University would be part of the event. The huge flat screens and mega speakers outside for all to experience. How the songs would transition seamlessly. When the "Animals" would appear (see them at 3:14 in previous link , when the "sky full of stars" would happen, (see this at 3:23 in previous link).

Where the stars would be ejected from, where the drone would need to be when that happened, and on and on and on.

T minus five seconds!

Stephen departs Keflavik International Airport, travels nineteen hundred miles and lands Pisa International Airport, Pisa Italy. Twenty-six miles later by Uber, he arrived Forte dei Marmi, Italy.

The "blind man" was expecting him.

Chapter Fourteen

Sister realized; she did not yet receive the visitor that the Boxman had said to expect. Time was not on anyone's side. A Physician was called to see the Boxman. Sister had alerted the girls who were now there with her. Stephen was on "Radio Silence" since he entered that helicopter. No one had heard anything from him. When the Doctor arrived, he could be seen examining the Boxman. When he was done, they had a private conversation. The Boxman asked him how long he had. The Doctor looked at him lovingly and said, "Not long". Are all your affairs in order? Yes, all except one. I need to be at the Governor's Ball, first Saturday of December. We'll do everything we can to make that happen. Yes, but nothing more. Also, Doctor, for how long would you guess I can continue my "Work"? For as long as you're able. That's something only you will know. Some people still need me. Marcie and Dawn entered as he left. Dawn translated. How are my two best girls? You know we won't be together much longer.

> *Marcie, that dance you told me about*
> *at the Governor's Ball and invited me*
> *to..., I plan on being there!*

The girls had already signed the documents to handle the final directives of the Boxman. He had no one else to ask. His wife had died three years ago. The girls were named, during a meeting with the Boxman's Attorney a week ago. They would now co-direct his medical needs and become co-executors when the time arrived. He had already executed a medical directive in their presence including a, "Do Not Resuscitate" clause and declining of any "advanced" care. In private, he gave the girls knowledge of his final wishes. He asked them if they wouldn't mind placing a sign downtown saying, "The Boxman will return tomorrow morning". They did.

There was still no sign pertaining to the Palliative-Hospice Center. They were still awaiting the final licensure. No one had any idea what was going on in the basement of McAuley. Sister had decided at the outset, that the Boxman could not wait for paperwork and placed in motion, his full care. Everyone routinely noticed Nursing students entering via the new ramp and back door. The entire Nursing department was sworn to secrecy. So, three times a day, three students in their scrubs, entered the "Center", not to be seen again for eight hours. The other two beds would remain unfilled until the license arrived.

Stephen reappears. Three days after he had left, he entered Miley and immediately kissed the two girls on their cheeks. Where have you been? Family business. Important family business that could not wait. My Father needed my help with a business venture and met me there. It required immediate attention. Where did you go? See that Ocean out there, as he pointed to the Atlantic Ocean just a few hundred yards away. To the other side and back. "That's all you can say?" Yup!

He finished breakfast and immediately met Katherine. Stephen, while you were gone, I've been thinking non-stop. We've come to realize, that it is fun to do the impossible and it has been my great honor to have helped you. I've been constantly reviewing the videos we have taken up until now. I noticed something in your dance that concerns me. What? You're not "Feeling" the Music. You're not "fluid" like Marcie. What do you mean? Did you hear what I just said? Stephen, you're not "Feeling" the music. Let me say that another way! You are not "feeeeeeeeeeling" the music!

I was literally awake all last night. I mean literally. I was very wrong about a hypothesis I had. I was on Cliff Walk, from two till five this morning and never went home. Stephen noticed she looked a little disheveled and he knew this was leading to something serious. Stephen, we are attempting to do the impossible and that will call for extraordinary strategies. As I walked Cliff Walk, for three hours under the full moon, I'd occasionally stop, lean against the wall and close my eyes. I'd listen to the rhythm of the waves. Stephen, I have a Doctor of Dance from Ohio State University which took me five years. I truthfully thought I knew everything necessary to turn you from a football player into a dancer. I tested my hypothesis over and over and last night I realized, I'd been very wrong. That occurred to me as I was listening to the rhythm of the waves, the "fluid motion" of the waves. Stephen, I am embarking on a new method of learning for you which I hope will compliment what you have learned so far. I haven't thought this hard about Dance since Graduate School. It has totally consumed me. I realized as I listened to the waves, that football is not a series of short dances. It is a game of violent contact. Just the opposite of dance. Helmets attempt to minimize the brain sloshing around inside your skull. It is a game involving gross kinetic energy being dissipated against an opposing player in a split second. The result can produce catastrophic, life changing injuries and occasionally death. That's not dance. Katherine was fomenting another Doctoral Thesis in her mind. Dance is about a shared purpose. Fluidity, a common, not opposing goal. A *gentle* release of chemical energy. Katherine's PhD studies had a strong focus on human anatomy and the body's ability to store and utilize chemical energy for muscle movement. She understood all the chemical pathways. How the body uses stored chemical energy to convert to heat and motion. The use of adenosine triphosphate (ATP) to power the contraction of muscles. The chemical pathways of creatine phosphate, glycogen and aerobic respiration to continuously produce ATP to power muscle contraction during prolonged exertion. Katherine was sharing all of this in laymen's terms with Stephen. He did not understand where this was all leading. My goal is to give you an idea of how the human body can dance and how its precise ability to control muscle contraction makes dance beautiful! Marcie understands this, but you don't.

Stephen, I have already been with a colleague of mine this morning from the Department of Chemistry and Biochemistry. We talked for two hours about our problem. He has agreed to help us. When I was a child, my Dad had a pocket watch. I'd be thrilled when we sat together, and he would open the back cover. I was mystified by its workings and motion. I'd often get out a magnifying glass to watch the moving symphony. As I got older, Dad began to explain to me the source of energy and its gradual dissipation to move the time keeping element and the dials to keep time. It was confusing at first, but I eventually understood. He taught me about the storage of potential energy in the Main Spring and the escapement gear used to gradually and precisely release some of the stored energy to power the process. He taught me how *jewels* were used to greatly minimize friction between moving parts. I always remembered those lessons, because, even at an early age, I thought of that pocket watch as dancing. It appeared alive. You will be seeing Professor McBride each day till further notice from two till three. Go into town and purchase a pocket watch. Preferably an heirloom piece from the 1800's. There are several stores to choose from and see Dr. McBride at two o'clock.

Stephen, I am Professor McBride. It is a pleasure to meet you. Please call me Bill. Do you have the watch? Here it is. Let's open it up. Wow! I've never seen anything like it. I can't believe that. Stephen, I have set up a microscope with a video screen. Let's look. Katherine has a theory. She believes, that if I teach you how this timepiece works, it will help you understand dance. I must say, her theory intrigues me. So, let's test her little hypothesis. Stephen, what you are watching is a symphony of motion. In its day, a watch such as this was the pinnacle of timekeeping. It is still a marvel today. People like you, who were born into the digital age, have absolutely no idea what a "Timepiece" is. Timepieces such as this, saved lives. Train conductors could now synchronize time with other trains to make sure they were not on the same track at the same time. It was a huge leap in technology. Stephen, tell me what you see. It's alive! Everything is moving with such precision. It's almost impossible to understand. You mean like the muscles of the human body, that can be so precisely controlled during Dance? Uh, Ya. What else? I see what looks like a spring and there are quite a few gears. And so... his lessons began.

Stephen, this new method of mine is just part of a multi-pronged approach to accomplish the impossible. This situation calls for drastic measures. I'm trying to compress a lifetime's worth of Dance into a month and a half. Truthfully, I don't know if that's possible. My brain says no, but my heart is willing to give it a try.

Do you know what a Tens Unit is? You mean a "Transcutaneous Electrical Nerve Stimulator"? You know how many times I've worn one for football injuries? O.K. then. Go get one, (I already have one) and wear it as long as you can and as high up as you can tolerate. What for? I want you to play the two songs repeatedly with headphones while you have the Tens Unit on. Move the pads from place to place but always have them on your legs. Use all four pads. No more running. Just walk around or dance around while listening to the songs. Let's see if we can't get you to "Feel" the music. For the next three days, he did so, for as long as he could. He would go to the area behind Breaker's Mansion, along the water, where the girls had taken him during his sensory deprivation. As people would sit on the granite bench or stand watching, Stephen would stand atop the marble wall overlooking the precipice and the Ocean below. And he'd dance. Often with his eyes closed! Oh, did he dance. Walkers would linger for long periods of time watching. He was dancing the dance. Of course, no one could hear the music. Students passing by were bewildered. Where did he learn to dance? How does he dance so well? Everyone knew Stephen.

Stephen, now do you know what I mean by feeling the music? I didn't know the human body could do that. Well, now you know. Put the music on, turn the volume way up and dance for me. She realized her little experiment had helped but not with complete success. Doctor McBride has brought something to my attention. He consulted with a Physics Professor who bought something, potentially miraculous, to my attention. This could be the Holy Grail. Dr. Williamson called in a lot of favors to obtain this. You have no freaking idea! This is a device which is still experimental. He had a friend send us this prototype. It was developed with input from Deaf people including singer Mandy Harvey. Do you know her? I know she's a Deaf singer but I'm not familiar with her music. I'm sure Marcie is. It's developed by "Not Impossible Labs" and is referred to as the "Music Not Impossible Project". "It includes a technology packed cargo vest and ankle and wrist bands. The suit translates sounds into a cascade of vibrations with different instruments registering in different zones across the ankles, wrists, back or rib cage". "It's already been tested at concerts and is a game changer for the Deaf." "The goal is to use only vibrations in order to feel, rather than hear music". God willing, "Deaf people will no longer have to stand close to speakers or squeeze a balloon to feel vibrations during a concert". Stephen, put this on! *(You absolutely must watch this video.)* It includes Mandy Moore and is subtitled for the Deaf! It's called a "Wireless Ecosystem". She had never taken such brazen approaches to dance but realized it was fun to do the impossible. Put the music on! Now his flow improved, and he entered the same trance-like state as Marcie did, and, was lost in Dance. He had crossed his very own Threshold of Hope.

Stephen, dance, dance, dance!

We are running out of time!

Be Marcie. Do you understand me? Be Marcie!

She lost her professional composure and screamed at him. Stephen, become Marcie, be part of her, become one with her. Become one with her!!! Be in a yolk with her!

Do you understand?

This has been my freaking goal for the last two months!

Be one with her!!!

Chapter Fifteen

The Boxman was back on America's Cup. Lines were as long as ever. Several hours now. Sister made a special visit. It was during this visit that the Boxman revealed to Sister who he was.

She said... oh!..., now I understand!

The two talked for thirty minutes or so. Sister told him not to worry about his final affairs as the

University would take care of many of those matters. He spoke in detail of his profound affection for Marcie, Dawn, and Stephen. Sister knew things concerning the "Triplets" which only she and the Boxman knew. His hands shook terribly as she held them. Please talk to Stephen about the matter which most concerns me. Don't worry, I will, and don't worry, I know he will. He kissed her hands and Sister placed the palms of her hands on his cheeks and kissed him on the head.

Later that day, Stephen arrived at Sister's office. Stephen, how is the plan going? So far as I can tell, very well. Is there anything I can do for you? There is one thing. Would you go with me and help me pick out a dress for Marcie to wear for the dance? I know what she plans on wearing from Katherine. She's been wearing it for years, but she doesn't have money for a new one. I'd love to help you with that.

Stephen, speaking of money, I called you here to ask you something. The Boxman is very worried about something. I want to alleviate that concern for him so he can leave us, in Peace. It concerns Marcie and Dawn. This is his concern… See if you can help him with that. Speak with your Father and let me know. I'll let me know right now! Consider it done. Please let the Boxman know "it is done!".

Except when Marcie was around, Dawn and Stephen signed whenever they were together, and they continued to meet late at night. He was making game tapes. Dawn thought she had acquired ASL at a rapid pace, but Stephen's intellect surpassed even hers. Marcie had already confronted Stephen after she had seen him in McKillop Library. All he said, in sign was, "I'm working on something". She signed to him, "like the helicopter"? But he did not grasp the last word she signed. So, she signed it again. This time slower. The right hand sitting on the thumb of the left and fluttering. He got it. He signed back, "Yes, like the helicopter". Marcie continued to see him in the "Little Room". He now faced another direction so she could not see his hands.

When Dawn met him that evening for instruction, he told her he had something to share with her. He told her (even though they had agreed that everything had to be signed) that it would take him a week to sign everything. She gave him a pass.

So, he began, and talked for the next two hours. She sat with a look of bewilderment the whole time. He revealed the entire "Grand Plan". It all started with the lightning bolt to his jaw. He said his teeth still hurt when he chewed. He thanked her sincerely. He revealed the purpose of his time with Katherine. All the help he was receiving from Sister, the University and his Father. He explained the teaching concerning the mask, the ear protectors and the cane. Everything about the helicopter and Reykjavik. His "side-trip" to Forte dei

Marmi, Italy. The bands and the choreography. ASL and his change of Major, his constant dancing, every detail.

Dawn was stunned!

She told him that no one had ever done anything like this for Marcie.

She never had a boyfriend, never went to "Prom". He shared about his deep relationship with the Boxman and the fact that he knew everything about the Plan. He revealed how he would ask Marcie for the dance and how nervous he would be about her reply. The very last thing he shared was the dress that Sister helped him select. Dawn, this is where you come in. As you know, except for Sigma Phi Sigma, students are not allowed to the Governor's Ball. Sister, as you would expect, has made an exception. You will be at the Governor's Ball. Please invite your parents. I'd love to meet them. Do you know anything about Marcie's parents? Her Mother died three years ago, and I haven't seen her father in some time. I'll try and contact him. About the dress. I've planned for Marcie's arrival at Ochre, where she will go, when, how and who will dress her and how she will proceed down the Grand Staircase and when I will ask her. Sister knows all these things. You will be the last person to give her away for the dance.

Silence! Neither said anything.

Tears welled up in Stephen's eyes as he said,

Dawn...I want to thank you for everything you have done for me. You helped change my life! Stephen, I have never heard of such Compassion and Affection. I am proud to have met you. Dawn... you and Marcie are the sisters I never had. You both mean the world to me.

Stephen... Marcie will never be the same.

She wiped the tears from his cheeks,

and both walked to their dorms in complete silence.

What more could be said. Marcie stirred when Dawn came in and signed, late night tutoring? Yes!

Chapter Sixteen

Dance, ASL, the Plan, the Boxman, Marcie, Dawn. Stephen's brain was beginning to swirl. He seemed to be in a trance wherever he would go. He could be seen and heard murmuring to himself. When he was in the company of his football friends, they realized he was not right. He couldn't focus. He'd just eat his food and occasionally catch what someone said. When someone said something to him, he'd react only if he heard his name but did not know what had just been said. For all their disagreements, the "Team" members were growing concerned. In mixed company his roommate said, Stephen are you O.K.? Ya. But they knew differently. He was not the person they knew. Not by a long shot. Their biggest concern was his lack of attention and inability to focus. That evening, out of legitimate concern, his roommate said, Stephen, there is mental health care available on Campus. Thanks, I'm O.K. I'll be back to normal, soon. Very soon!

Stephen, look at me! Katherine knew. He was looking at her but literally through her. She had not regained her composure since the time she screamed at him to be in Marcie's yolk, to be one with her. Kathrine knew, he was close to maxing out. That didn't matter now. She'd be no different than his screaming coaches. He'd always been able to handle that she thought! Stephen, this is for all the marbles. The goal line is in sight. Do you freaking hear me? Silence... he was shaking. You wanted to do the impossible, yes? You are almost there. Stephen looked towards the window and a blank stare came over him.

He continued so for about one minute as Katherine looked on. She knew something profound, maybe dangerous was occurring.

Stephen's game tape was focused on Falcon Heavy. He was playing back the tape of when the vehicle reached "Max-Q". Max-Q, as he well knew, was the point when the "Maximum Dynamic Pressure", the largest amount of aerodynamic stress, was exerted on the vehicle. Even though he was still at T-5 seconds, he was at his own Max-Q. He regained his focus and said to Katherine, **let's do this!** In a sense, he realized that at Max-Q, one of only two things could happen. Either he'd implode or continue in flight. This brought him some relief as he realized he'd not imploded.

Katherine screamed, "do this Stephen, get the fucking touchdown". This will be way different than "All-22", this will be "All-800", with thousands more watching this stream live. He already knew that the University Board of Trustees had arranged for a news helicopter to stream the event live from Reefe Hall, and into Ochre Court. No doubt this would be a marketing opportunity that money could not buy. The local news station would interrupt broadcasting to stream live. Stephen knew all this, and it contributed to his Max-Q. But truth be told, he was used to this sort of thing from football. He also knew, this was different.

Stephen, what did you learn from Dr. McBride?

I don't know where to begin. After Bill taught me all about the physics involved in timepieces, we eventually took the whole thing apart. I have never used such tiny tools.

It was only then that I understood. I put it back together with Bill's help and it "Sprung back to Life"! And how does that relate to dance? I realized that the human body works in an unimaginable way. Our muscle cells store the energy used to contract our muscles. Muscles use ATP to power the whole affair and to produce ATP on the fly, during prolonged physical exertion. ATP releases that energy, as a mainspring does in a watch. So, Stephen, what is the difference between a mechanical device and a human? He thought for a moment. A watch doesn't have a brain. I realized my body will only do what my brain tells it to do. That if my dance is not to Marcie's level, I have only myself to blame. That's it!

That evening Katherine pushed him relentlessly. He drew upon a deep well of Hope. No matter what she screamed he responded. Scream, scream, and scream. This was T minus one week by Katherine's clock!

Katherine was on fire. She took both her hands and placed them firmly on his cheeks. She screamed, Stephen, you're almost there, almost there. Stay focused...

be Marcie, be in her yolk, be coupled to her, be one with her.

And, one other thing. This is your final assignment! Every single day, from here on in, you are to sit for at least one hour or more in Our Lady of Mercy Chapel. There you will receive your final instruction.

Katharine's hands returned to her sides and Stephen staggered out into the cold air.

Aerial lift trucks could be seen outside of O'Hare Academic Center (home of Nursing department), McKillop Library, Ochre Court and Miley Hall. They were running cables up the sides to the roof.

Then they lifted what looked to be lights of some sort. In fact, they were high intensity halogen "Follow- Spot" lights, from the Theatre Department. Huge flat screens and speakers were being erected in front of the portico and main entrance to Ochre Court. People were curious. Maybe for the Governor's Ball? No one really knew why. Activity was beginning to ramp up at Ochre Court and McAuley Hall. Trucks came and went.

The Boxman was becoming more and more ill as the days went by. Nursing students volunteered to stay with him at all times on America's Cup.

Stephen stumbled over to Mercy Chapel after he left Katherine. Dawn bumped into him. She told Stephen she had no luck contacting Marcie's Father. His phone number has been disconnected and I have no other contact information. I can't ask Marcie! She'll know something's up. Maybe she already contacted him? I'll just ask her if he's coming. Would be a shame if he wasn't there.

Stephen saw the aerial lift trucks but paid no attention. He had been "The" man about campus for months now but suddenly felt all alone. He knew most of the campus extremely well but had never set foot in Mercy Chapel. He had been there for some time when the University Chaplain noticed him with his head buried deeply in his hands. He did not see or hear Father coming. **Father, knelt by his side in the aisle** and said to Stephen...,

"Are you O.K.?"

Not really Father. I need to ask you something. Father, can you hear my confession? Stephen, (Father knew who he was), let's do it right here.

Stephen hadn't made a confession since his Confirmation and Father was extremely Compassionate to him. After a half hour or so, Stephen was done. Father said the words he desperately needed to hear. "Stephen, I absolve you from your sins, in the name of the Father and the Son and the Holy Spirit. Amen"

Stephen thanked him profusely and left Mercy Chapel having received Mercy. Stephen's back! Oh, is he back!

All the way to his dorm room in Young, he said to every single person he encountered. "Hey! Have a great day!" Stephen was better than back. He continued, as he'd been doing all along. Running, dancing, ASL with Dawn, visiting Mercy Chapel, lessons at night, visiting the Boxman, Dawn and Marcie. Marcie had no clue what was going on, with her full devotion centered on her dance routine. She had no idea her world would irreversibly change by week's end.

Chapter Seventeen

There was lots of activity down in Newport Harbor. Difficult to miss. A familiar Mega Yacht had been at anchor for some time now. Not that a Mega Yacht was a rare occasion for Newport, but they tended to come and go. Yachts this length could not possibly find dock space as they were simply too long. They would anchor in harbor and be serviced by tenders. Funny thing though. People saw small barges coming and going from this yacht and unloading large amounts of boxes. Large amounts of stuff were also leaving the Yacht on their return trips to shore. You could clearly make that out. There were several very large dumpsters on shore that were routinely taken, emptied, and returned. Locals were especially intrigued. In the morning you could see twenty or so workers, with tool belts, boarding the first barge of the day. This was happening every day for some time now. People that "Yacht Watch", already knew the particulars of this yacht by "Googling" the name on its bow. It was a 350-foot vessel valued at 110 million dollars. But then something interesting happened. Very large tarps were draped over both sides of the bow of the ship. And, so this continued, every day, regardless of weather.

Stephen, Marcie and Dawn became especially attentive to the Boxman. Since Stephen did not attend classes anymore, he routinely walked the Boxman to and fro. His Doctor had convinced him to cut back on his "Work", so new hours were posted on the "Box" reading, 9:00 to 3:00. Far less than originally. There were days Stephen stayed all day along with the Student Nurse volunteers. He got to know some of them quite well. When Stephen was there, he always insisted on taking the Boxman to the restroom and could often be seen feeding him as well. There was a lot of conversing between the two any chance they had. Stephen would wipe his face and hands after feeding him and affectionately take him back to his box. The Parkinson's was manifesting itself in profound ways now.

The Boxman was first diagnosed with Early Onset Parkinson's Disease, (EOPD) at thirty-five years old, according to his chart at McAuley Hall. **His chart had no last name!** The dysphagia made it difficult for him to swallow and drooling was constant. Dyskinesia (involuntary, erratic writhing movements of the face, arms, legs, or trunk) and bradykinesia (slowness of movement) were exceedingly bad as was the resting tremor and rigidity. Let's not forget that little brain tumor. Studies indicate that the risk of developing a brain tumor is significantly higher in patients with Parkinson's than without. Now it was a race to the finish line.

The Ball! You could not help but notice the deep affection Stephen had for him. Although Stephen named him the Boxman in one of his rages, for whatever reason, the name stuck and was always used reverently. Even the Boxman referred to himself as such. They had already had a significant number of personal conversations, both during their walks and at home in McAuley. Just one day prior, a new sign with the "Salve" logo appeared near the street outside of McAuley.

It read,

> ***Mercy Palliative-Hospice Center,***
> ***Department of Nursing.***
>
> ***Thanks! to an Anonymous Donor***
>
> *Everyone took notice!*

Sister came to the Boxman every day now. She did not wait in line but would come and kneel in front of him. She always held his hands and Stephen could hear her asking him how he was doing and whether he needed anything. Stephen was witnessing Compassion straight up. He heard her say to him..., "We good on the Ball?" God willing Sister.

I can't disappoint Marcie.

She's hoping, I'll honor her invitation.

How can I disappoint an Angel?

Mark, I'll pray that you receive that gift. This was a revelation to Stephen. He had never known or heard the Boxman's name. Mark!

On the walk back "Home" that afternoon, the Boxman asked Stephen if he needed anything from him. Just what you would expect of him. Stephen said, "All systems were ready for launch". He asked him about Marcie and Dawn. Everything had been taken care of with his Father's eager help. The Boxman knew all the details of the Plan, even though Stephen did not know something about the Boxman. Between Sister, the Boxman and Stephen, the grand finale was approaching.

T-4.   Brass Attack, Rihanna, Coldplay (done). Equipment already arriving, accommodations at The Viking, lighting/sound, Ochre Point Avenue, Security, limousines, the Dress, Private jet from London (done)

The Football Team and Sigma Phi Sigma, Special Guests. Dawn, his attire. (Done)

Special arrangements for the Boxman, (Done)

Final check of Drone GPS for maintaining a fixed altitude and location, (Done)

Sky Full of Stars and "Animals", (done)

Media and helicopter with GPS coordinates, (done)

Final rehearsals with Katherine, (ongoing)

Visits to Mercy Chapel, (ongoing)

ASL with Dawn, (Ongoing)

Meetings with Sister and the Boxman, (ongoing)

Running and Dancing, (ongoing)

Arrangements for messaging boards on America's Cup and Ochre Point Avenue (done)

Huge flat screens and speakers at front of Ochre Court, (done)

Oh, my God!

Space-X Falcon Heavy go for launch.

Falcon Heavy is configured for flight.

T-3: Core Stage Ignition Sequence Start.

Chapter Eighteen

Did you tell Sister to expect me? Yes, I have. This was the final visit of the "Yacht Man". He'd already visited the Boxman three times prior. When you call her office, just say that "You are a friend of the Boxman". She will know. I'll need to see her the day of the Ball. That will not be a problem. I'll let her know.

The Boxman's disease was now "Stage Five". He suffered from dyspnea, (difficulty breathing), his speech was becoming unintelligible; he could not eat or drink sufficiently, was becoming incontinent with insomnia. He could still hear and did not have dementia. He was failing fast and now on portable oxygen monitored closely by the Nursing Students. Sister called Stephen, Marcie and Dawn to the "Center". The Dean met them to discuss his situation. All agreed that his care was rapidly shifting from Palliative to Hospice. They would do all they could to protect his final wish... The Ball. It was only two days away. That evening, after all three walked him home, Sister had a private conversation with him. They agreed that tomorrow would be his last day of "Work". The Boxman had been mentally and spiritually preparing for this time. He was a man of deep spirituality and had been doing his own homework ever since his diagnosis and increasingly as time went by. He asked Sister to send Father to see him. I'll do that Mark.

Hello Mark, Sister sent for me. How are you my Brother? As well as I can be Father. I'm preparing to cross my final "Threshold of Hope". I know you are. You have prepared well.

Mark, how can I help you? Father hear my Confession.

...Mark, through the ministry of the Church, may God give you pardon, and peace and I absolve you of your sins, in the name of the Father, Son and Holy Spirit, Amen.

Then Father laid his hands on his head and anointed his forehead and palms with the Holy Oil of the sick. His final Sacrament.

Mark, your "Work" amongst us will never be forgotten. Your good example of Mercy and Compassion will be with this University always.

The Boxman's last day of work!

The line was long as usual. He pleaded to be taken to America's Cup at 7:00 A.M. All three took him there. Stephen stayed all day. He watched and watched and watched the Boxman. Tears welled up in Stephen's eyes all day. Pacing back and forth he did not speak to anyone. He was witnessing the end of a heroic journey. It took great effort for the Boxman to extend his frail arm to give each guest a touch on their heads and a final message. In all the time he did his "Work" he did nothing but listen. Never once corrected anyone. Just accepted everything about each Soul that came to visit. He would only speak a sentence or two to each person, conveying some important message. Just like Stephen's visit with Father in the Chapel, each left the Boxman with a renewed spirit. It was visible and Stephen was focused in on that all day. About 4:00, he did all he could do. There were still people in line as Stephen approached him. Stephen said to those in line, the Boxman needs to go home. All could see and understand. He was dying. As Stephen wrapped him in a blanket and began to wheel him away with Dawn and Marcie, the people in line began to clap and weep and others, including numerous store merchants, joined them along America's Cup. Everyone had come to know the Boxman. They knew he would not return.

That evening Stephen had his final class with Katherine. He just finished up his final run and appeared drenched in sweat. Stephen, how is the Boxman? Preparing to go home. Will he make the Ball? He has run a race far greater than me. He'll make it.

Did you receive your "Final Instruction" at Mercy Chapel? I have. Would you like to share it with me? Yes.

Katherine, many times you said to me that I needed to be in the same "Yolk" as Marcie. Be one with her. Be her. I was completely unfamiliar with the concept of a "Yolk". That bothered me a lot. I looked it up in Matthew and online. I'd just sit and think about that passage. The first thing I learned was that, only similar animals can be in a "Yolk", together. It doesn't work well otherwise. I realized I had to be "similar" to Marcie. What was revealed to me next was deeply moving! It's the part that says, "For I am gentle and humble of heart". I focused in on that, because I never thought of myself that way, but always thought that way of Marcie. I was ashamed of myself. How could I be in a "Yolk" with Marcie, if I myself, was not "gentle and humble of heart"? This bothered me a lot.

When I would run, I constantly thought about that. I'd be dancing on Cliff Walk and meditate on that. I had never meditated before, unless you include football. This is different. Things were "revealed" to me. Deep things. I knew I had never been gentle and humble of heart. This was disturbing to me.

As I watched the Boxman during his final day of "Work", I realized that he was gentle and humble of heart. I realized that it was being shown to me.

My eyes opened and I was deeply affected by that.

This is the message I received. Stephen, I could have never taught you that. Wisdom such as that is entirely a gift from a higher power. Be thankful for that gift!

Now, **be** Marcie...dance!

What Katherine would witness next was beyond words. It was "The Dance", Marcie's dance! Stephen was in a trance like state. OMG, OMG. When he was finished, he was completely spent, just like Marcie. He just stood there as Katherine looked at him. She just looked at him.

She walked up to him…

and put the palms of both hands on his cheeks.

Stephen…it's been fun to do the impossible! You're ready!

Chapter Nineteen

Text from Sister. Marcie are you ready? Yes Sister. You will arrive at my office exactly at 9:45 tomorrow. Dawn will be waiting for you outside Ochre Court. Is there anything you need? No, I'm good. Your Dance will be at 10:00 sharp. O.K.

Phone rings in Sister's Office and she answered. Sister, I am a friend of the Boxman. I need to speak with you. Yes, the Boxman said you'd be in touch. Where are you now? Down at the Harbor. Come right over.

Do you know where to find me? Second floor of Ochre Court. Yes, I know. I'll be there in ten minutes. Park under the portico and if anyone asks, tell them Sister said to do so. A nondescript gentleman entered Sister's Office. He announced himself as the Boxman's friend and shook Sister's hand. He began by asking her if she had an hour or so to spare. Of course. I need you to take a walk with me down to the Harbor. Where the Boxman used to be. Get your coat, it's cold outside. They left Ochre Court heading to the Harbor. Sister, I have a confession to make. I am a very wealthy man. I'm not sure if that's a blessing or a curse. For quite some time now, I've come to believe it is a curse. I've sailed around this world many times, always imagining the next sail would bring me Peace. But that quest has been futile. I am a miserable man. How can a man as wealthy as me be so miserable? For all my wealth I've never done anything like the Boxman. Imagine him..., "Free Help". The first time I saw his sign it struck a chord with me. I've never done anything for free. I needed help. Here was a man who is gravely ill and totally happy, and here I am, one of the wealthiest men on earth and I'm miserable. I went to see him. I poured out my soul. He said just one sentence to me. I went back twice more. Everywhere I go, people point at me and say, hey, isn't he...I began thinking. I've spent the last two months researching everything Salve. I've been to this port many times. It is one of my most favorite places on earth. On my journeys, across the oceans, I've seen firsthand the environmental catastrophes of our oceans. I've sailed through "The Great Pacific Garbage Patch" multiple times. It is the largest accumulation of ocean plastic in the world located between Hawaii and California. There is another one called the North Atlantic Garbage Patch. What's even worse is the amount of "Micro-plastics". There's more micro-plastics below the surface than we see on the surface. They've invaded the deep ocean and the food chain. This has greatly dismayed me. I'm not bright enough to know what I could possibly do, even with my great wealth. This is for young minds to figure out, and they will. They were now on Memorial Boulevard heading for America's Cup. Sister just listened. I began to give thought to the advice of the Boxman. I've thought long and hard. What he said to me, I realized was true. So, I began to realize that I could possibly do something about the oceans' desperate situation. They were now on America's Cup. During the night, his little boat had pulled up anchor and was now as close to shore as its draft would allow. Sister had listened, as the Boxman had, to this kind gentleman's story. Suddenly, he said to Sister, we're here. Sister was confused. She looked around but did not see anything out of the ordinary. She had seen the same boat, with the big tarps across the bow, on her frequent visits to the Boxman. She noticed it was lots closer, situated parallel to shore. But other than that, nothing else jumped out at her. He said to Sister, I am heeding, the "Good Counsel", of the Boxman. Salve is uniquely situated on the Atlantic Ocean. I want you… to help me… by helping our world's oceans. He made a hand gesture to the yacht. At that, a great horn emanated from it. It blew non-stop until the tarps were pulled back from the bow. Sister just stood there. Nothing in her life had prepared her for this. She was silent.

Across the bow, in huge letters. "Salve Regina University-Department of Oceanography". He had a large manila envelope which he asked her to open. She did. He said to her, this is the deed to this ship. It has been outfitted with state-of-the-art laboratories. There is a thirty-million-dollar check to endow your new Department with necessary funds for long term upkeep and expenses of the boat. I have hired a local Captain and crew. Additionally, I have set up a fifty-million-dollar Trust Fund. It is unrestricted. The interest can be utilized any way you wish. Scholarships perhaps? The Yachtsman was well acquainted with another philanthropist by the name of Alfred Nobel and the Nobel Prizes. Having invented dynamite and amassing a huge fortune he was subsequently referred to as "The Merchant of Death". He left his entire fortune, to reward ...

those who serve Humanity.

This gift has given me joy I've been searching for! The Boxman said just one sentence to me each of my three visits. The first was, "You might want to consider giving away the things that don't bring you joy". Secondly, "the view from the top can get a little hazy". Lastly, "it might be time to come down from the ladder". I took his advice. Sister was speechless. Aside from the gift of Ochre Court itself, this was now the largest gift the University ever received, by far. She just hugged him.

Are you coming to the Ball tonight? I wasn't planning on that as I'm flying out in the morning. Please, be my personal guest? The kids tell me I can dance! Under one condition. If you mention this in any way, do not mention my name or point me out. Will the Boxman be there? Yes... Thank him!

Agreed.

The two message boards on America's Cup and Ochre Point Avenue had been illuminated the day before. They read, "Be part of Salve history. Ochre Point Avenue, this Saturday 9:00 P.M." Then it flashed to read, "parking and shuttle from William S. Rogers High School".

T-1!

Marcie had dressed in the same dance outfit as she had since High School. She had no sense of what was occurring outside. She walked out of Reefe at 9:35. She wore a heavy winter coat and looked no different than anyone else. It snowed that day and there were about four inches, beautifully blanketing everything. She was startled in a big way. There was a single "Follow Spot" light, beaming from the roof of O'Hare Academic Center focused directly onto Reefe Hall. She could not grasp that. Marcie also saw a helicopter on the lawn outside of McKillop. What the heck? But that was not all. People were arriving in droves all along Ochre Point Avenue. Hundreds... then thousands. Flashing lights were everywhere. Ochre Point Avenue was completely blocked off from Sheppard Avenue to Webster Street. There were no parked cars the entire length. She was dumb struck. Never in a million years did she imagine this had anything to do with her. All she knew was what the message boards read about being "part of Salve history". Since she was a freshman, she imagined that all of this was just part and parcel of the Governor's Ball. Wow, she thought.

At this same time, Stephen was with the Boxman. The Nursing Students already had him dressed in a tuxedo. Stephen asked him for a final blessing. The Boxman placed both his shaking hands upon his head and said...**"May the Spirit of God rest upon You!"** The Pre-Ball alumni event had already concluded at McAuley and the Ball was well on its way at 8:00. Brass Attack was playing their heart out and the dance floor was crammed. Food, drinks, everywhere. The most beautiful Christmas tree sat adjacent to the Grand Staircase. Ochre Court was packed from floor to ceiling, six hundred plus. Women wore the finest dresses and men were dressed to the nines. Everything was simply exquisite. Marcie weaved her way through the throngs and to the great gate of Ochre Court which reads, "Salve Regina University". She'd seen that sign many times. Something was different tonight. Below that sign hung another that read, "I have a dream"

(See Sky Full of Stars video at 1:25)

She had seen the trees illuminated with a spectacular brilliance for several nights but had not walked between them. She was now walking down the same gravel walkway that Stephen used when he was "blind". It was spectacular beyond words, as Ochre Court was illuminated as well. Dawn was waiting under the portico. When Marcie entered Ochre Court, she signed, Dawn, I have never seen anything like this! I know! She could "feel" the pulses from Brass Attack. It was now 9:45 as they walked up the Grand Staircase to the President's Office. The door was closed when they arrived. When they entered, they saw Sister, several nursing students and a large box with a bow on Sister's desk. Marcie was confused. She signed to Dawn, "What's going on?". Marcie, Sister has a special gift for you that she purchased with a friend's help. Go on...open it. She could not believe her eyes. The most amazing dance outfit she had ever seen. And spectacular dance shoes as well. Blazing canary yellow with black tassels on the shoulders and hem. Simply breathtaking! Girls...get her dressed. Sister left.

As soon as the girls had entered Sister's office, amazing things were suddenly happening downstairs. Brass Attack stopped playing and Sister took to the microphone. Of course, Marcie could not hear any of this. Dear friends, a once in a lifetime event is about to occur here at Salve. This was all streaming live (flat screens) to about three thousand people outside, about ten deep, lining Ochre Point Avenue, including every student from Salve. This has not happened before. I need to ask for your help. We need to have the entire dance floor cleared. Please relocate to the upstairs balconies. What you are about to witness will be Salve History in the making. Something I trust you have never seen. As she was saying this, the front glass doors opened and the entire football team entered, all in tuxedos. They and Sigma Phi Sigma already knew what to do. They lined the Grand Staircase beginning at the door to Sister's office, alternating each stair. Sigma Phi Sigma was in their "Official" attire. Outside, the helicopter, which had sat silent, now came to life. On its side read, "WPRI local news". It lifted off and perched itself, just high enough above Ochre Point Avenue, to prevent rotor wash on the crowd. Inside, things were feverish. All were now on the balconies and a sudden roar arose as everyone spotted Rihanna. She had arrived by a side door and was sequestered with her band in the "Dessert Room", OMG. Every cell phone came out. Next came an influx of people. These were all Special Guests, including Marcie's friends and teachers from ASD. Before Marcie had arrived, Dawn scoured the entire crowd for Marcie's father. She did not see him. The special guests encircled the dance floor except for the area at the bottom of the Grand Staircase. Only three people occupied that space. In the center was the Boxman in his wheelchair and Stephen and Dawn to each side. Dawn said to Stephen, I don't see Marcie's Dad. He must be here, she said he would be!

Stephen knew that he was!

Silence fell upon Ochre Court. The drone assumed its GPS location above the floor. "All-800"!

At exactly 9:56, Sister opened her office door. There was Marcie...perfection. Since Dawn was downstairs Sister had a handwritten note for Marcie. "Are you ready?" She nodded her head, yes. Sister walked her to the door. There was live video from multiple locations. On air, the screen was split into four quadrants. It was streaming live to WPRI, which had interrupted its broadcasting and to the crowd outside.

The first two football players each took one of her hands in one of theirs, as the next set of Sigma Phi Sigma hands set out to meet hers. Every two feet she was handed off to the next two persons. Marci's eyes darted everywhere. Halfway down the staircase she spotted the drone and then Rihanna. What was happening she thought? She immediately connected Rihanna to her song. She rounded the last curve of the Grand Staircase and stopped, still holding the hands of two former hyenas. She now saw the Boxman, Stephen, Dawn and all her friends. You could see tears in her eyes. She slowly proceeded down the remaining steps and found herself face to face with the Boxman, Stephen and Dawn. Dawn took both her hands in both of hers. She then placed Marcie's angelic hands in Stephen's, bent and kissed their "coupled" hands. Stephen was in tuxedo pants, a shirt, the same canary yellow, and a black bow tie but no jacket. Everything he'd planned, including the sign reading, "I have a dream", revolved around the answer to the next question. Thousands of miles of travel were on the line. One hundred and fifty thousand in expenses. Katherine and Sister's and the University's reputation. This was the greatest "Play" of his life. He released Marcie's hands and in perfect ASL he signed,

Dearest Marcie, may I have this... dance?

She had an immediate flashback to seeing him signing in McKillop, "Marcie may I have this".

She signed, Stephen...how is that possible?

Another flashback: The time she saw him with Katherine.

Cell phones were flashing everywhere, the drone hummed but there was dead silence. All stood still.

Stephen, how can you know the dance?

I do.

Stephen...let's do this!

Both Marcie and Stephen kissed the Boxman and Dawn on their cheeks. Marcie signed to Dawn,

"Bring him close, very close. Help hold his head up!"

"This is for him, I'm going all in, some place... I've never been!"

Stephen took Marcie by the hand and both stood in the center of the floor. Stephen signed,

"Marcie is your Dad here?" Yes!

I already saw him! Oh good!

It was pre-arranged that everything would not begin until Stephen gave the go ahead. That signal would be instantaneously relayed to Coldplay which would start immediately at Reefe.The songs were offset by twenty-four seconds at which time Rihanna would begin. All precisely choreographed in Reykjavik.

He took both her hands and looked at her with deep affection. Something flashed through his mind..., "For I am gentle and humble in heart". He released her hands and motioned to Rihanna. Coldplay started at Keefe.

All at once, the twelve "follow-spots" turned night into day. Doors opened in Reefe and out came Coldplay with their balloons, flowers, and bubble machine. They were playing "Sky Full of Stars". The Animals following. It was thunderous. The flat screens were now split between inside and outside. As planned, the speakers outside were bellowing, "A sky full of stars"

And twenty-four seconds later...in Ochre Court, was a brilliant flash of light followed by a crack of thunder. It began!

T-0, engine ignition.

"Hold-Down Clamps" secure till 5 million pounds of thrust, clamps release...

Liftoff of Falcon Heavy!

The music was thunderous; they were both in their trance, their bodies under the control of millions of neurons firing in perfect sequence. The human mind at Max-Q. The Human Spirit at Max-Q. They looked at each other only occasionally. Mostly their eyes were closed. They were both "feeling" the thunderous pulses. Such precision... jaw dropping. Hundreds of cell phones extended over the balconies. Their electrons now intertwined. They were on fire. A symphony of the human spirit. Millions of years of genetic code, bearing down. The universe, bearing down. A higher power, bearing down.

People were screaming, not believing.

The helicopter whirled but no one could hear it anymore. Just thousands going ballistic outside.

Inside complete pandemonium. The Boxman summoning every ounce of energy to take it all in. A smile as Dawn held his head up. She felt his tears on her hands. Sister glanced at Katherine who winked back at her.

They were now in an altered universe. Their bodies pulsating. Beauty beyond words. The musicians in perfect unison. No friction, feet barely touching the floor...

two "jewels".

Tassels twirling. Arms and hands doing things arms and hands can't do. The impossible was now possible!Their skin glistening.

Stephen's parents watching. Stunned!

Dawn's parents watching. Stunned!

Marcie's father...?

They ramped up and ramped up and ramped up more. Nothing could stop them. Muscle cells in maximum overload...

ATP on the fly!

Heavily perspiring as their bodies dumped heat. They were several minutes into, "We found Love". The pulses seemingly entering their bodies and exiting into the crowd. The sound level was increasing frequently as the sound mixer elevated the decibel level to just short of what a hearing person could tolerate. Measured at Reykjavik! Marcie felt this. Stephen felt this. Everyone felt this. Unbelievable volume, now pulsing out of control. The drone keeping watch.

Coldplay passes the Great Gate, the crowd following. All now jammed between the portico of Ochre, and Stonor and Drexel Halls. All going berserk. Doors still closed. Stephen and Marcie nearing the hand-off from Rihanna to Coldplay.

5-4-3, "We found Love", ends

Doors open, 2-1

Coldplay starts, "Sky full of Stars", round two.

Marcie and Stephen had time for just one deep breath. Marcie sees Coldplay. The Animals surround them. Coldplay just behind Dawn and the Boxman. Brass Attack in perfect unison.

They enter Nirvana.

They are now finally one, with each other and God.

They are in the same "Yolk". Three minds, three spirits, and three wills in perfect unison.

Stephen flashing back.

Be in her yolk, be one with her, be her!

You heard the call out.

Vehicle is now supersonic.

Past Max-Q.

Two minutes to go. Both open their eyes and they stay open. Sweat flying off their bodies. Tendons, muscles, heart, all Max-Q. Stephen and Katherine realize Marcie's entering a world neither had seen. Steps neither had seen.

She is on her own "event horizon",
the edge of a black hole.

One foot in, one out.

In a sky full of stars!

Stephen follows. Dance at a cosmic level. Stephen signs to her...go!

Marcie is now hypersonic, Mach 5.

Katherine mouths, OMG.

Stephen keeps up!

Almost spent... completely spent. Fifty seconds to go. The heavens open! Thousands of white paper "stars" explode from the top balcony. Animals going crazy. Stars sticking to Marcie and Stephen's drenched skin.

Fifteen seconds,

heavy panting.

Center and side booster reentry burn completed

...ATP exhausted.

Landing burns activated...

Landing legs deployed.

10...9...8...7...6...5...4...3...2...1

It's over!

The impossible has happened!

Marcie takes Stephen's hand...three steps; both kneel, take the Boxman's hands, and kiss him. One on each cheek.

Marcie "speaks" something to his ear.

The Falcon has landed!

Absolute Mayhem!!!

Chapter Twenty

Girls! Get him home, now!

Brass Attack played on. Sister motions to the Football Team and Sigma Phi Sigma to get out on the dance floor. She joins them as does the Yachtsman, Sister's partner. Others join them, shoulder to shoulder. Song after song, shoulder to shoulder. Dessert room now opens. Cake pops! Marcie and Stephen are mobbed. Stephen interprets! Marcie was witnessing Stephens excellent ASL for the first time. Rihanna and Coldplay make the rounds. Complete fun!

11:00 Sister takes the microphone.

Those of you who have attended the Governor's Ball in the past are aware that I always "announce" the proceeds of the Ball which you all know is used to fund scholarships for our great University. As usual, this year we have surpassed our record set last year. It gives me great honor to announce that the proceeds of this year's Ball are five hundred fifty thousand. Considering that, and in thanks for our historic evening, I am extending tonight's Ball till 1:00 A.M. But before that, I have one more announcement which I'd like the Governor to join me in making. She'd already been briefed by Sister. Friends, (her voice cracked), something happened today which has not happened in the history of Salve Regina University. Everyone who knew Sister had never, ever, seen her get emotional. Today, history was made, in addition to all that you have witnessed. Most of you have come to know or hear of the Boxman who was here tonight. Unfortunately, he is very ill and needed to go home.

The Boxman has brought great blessings to this University. He has bought Mercy, Compassion, Hope and Love to many, including myself. You could see Sister was on the verge of tears. At this moment, we stand in a building which for all these years has represented the largest single donation to this University, ever.

This morning someone appeared in my office. He was there as the result of his visits with the Boxman. He has chosen to remain anonymous. He walked me down to the Harbor to show me something. He told me, what he wanted me to see, was the result of three sentences the Boxman had said to him. Just three sentences! As the result of the Love and Compassion and Hope that the Boxman has shown our donor, I am announcing the following.

A ship sits in Newport harbor which is now the home of a new academic department, Salve Regina Department of Oceanography. This donor has endowed the department and yacht for many years to come. In addition, he has established a trust fund whose earnings will fund scholarships for that department and the entire University. It is an unrestricted trust. I don't know how to tell you this. There was a long pause. Sister was quivering. Our donor's gift to our wonderful University is now the largest in our history. His gift is in the amount of one-hundred-ninety-million dollars. You can see part of that gift in the Harbor as you leave tomorrow. Thank-you dear God!

Coldplay and Rihanna now left. They were all exhausted. Brass attack continued churning out big sound. Dance floor still packed. Cake pops all gone. Sister says to Stephen. Go to my office. In the bottom left hand drawer, you will find a box marked "Boxman". Get it, and Marcie and Dawn, and meet me back here. She found the Yachtsman and asked him to wait with her. When Stephen, Marcie, and Dawn appeared, she asked them all to follow her and the Yachtsman to the "Center". Stephen signed this to Marcie. They passed behind Mercy Chapel and down the ramp at McAuley. Sister said to the nursing students, how is he? Sister, he slipped into a coma. O.K. then.

Sister called two student nurses, as they all entered the room. She opened the box and took out two pieces of paper, copies of one another. She had the two student nurses read, sign and date both copies where it said "Witness". Then she handed one copy to Marcie to follow along. Inside the box was fabric. All surrounded the Boxman. Marcie and the Yachtsman each held one of his hands. Sister knew, the sense of hearing is thought to be the last sense to fail in the dying process.

She asked Dawn to hold her copy so she could read from it. She extended both hands over the Boxman, as a blessing, and read from the paper...

Mark, by the power of the President of Salve Regina University and the Board of Trustees, today I confer upon you the following:

This great University has witnessed, firsthand, your heroic practice of Mercy, Compassion, Hope and Love upon the City of Newport, the University of Salve Regina and others far and wide. Your "Work" has had an indelible impact upon this entire community. We have heard firsthand testimony of your unselfish service to mankind and your concern for the downtrodden and heartbroken. You have lived out your final days in service to all who have sought your wisdom and help. You have accomplished this while yourself suffering from an enormous affliction. You have single handedly espoused the doctrine of this University and brought to life the ideal of "Loving others as yourself". Your witness to "Truth" has inspired this University and all who possess

the innate desire to tend to the needs of their fellow man.

As a result, of your "Work" amongst the poor in spirit, you have changed lives. You yourself have placed your Trust and Confidence in God, rather than material possessions, and, your own health. For this we are eternally grateful.

As President of Salve Regina University, "I confer upon you the title of "Litterarum humanarum doctor" (L.H.D.), Doctor of Humane Letters.

Peace be granted unto you and may Perpetual Light shine upon you, Amen".

Marcie, take this "White Hood" and place it across Mark as a sign of the Doctor of Humane Letters. **Only four people knew, and one was dying.** Sister and the Yachtsman left. Marcie, Stephen and Dawn a while later. When they left, all was quiet. The Ball had ended. Dawn headed back to Keefe.

Stephen walked with his arm around Marcie, as a strong ocean wind had blown up, but not for that reason. They walked on Cliff Walk for the next hour and signed not a single word. When they arrived at Reefe, Stephen signed to Marcie, may I come in for just a few minutes? Sure. Dawn was sound asleep in the bedroom they shared. Stephen signed...May I tuck you in? Give me a few minutes to change.

She appeared wearing a pair of fuzzy bunny pajamas complete with hood and ears. They entered her room as Dawn was out cold. She got in bed and Stephen tenderly covered her. She signed, "Good night Stephen" ... "Good night Marcie". As he turned to leave, he felt a hand grab him. He turned around to Marcie. She signed to him. Stephen, I have something to tell you. You cannot tell anyone! Only two other people in the entire world know and that is Sister and the Boxman. As soon as I tell you, please leave, O.K.? O.K. She signed the secret. Stephen had to tell her. Marcie...I already knew several weeks ago. How? I can't tell you that now. I had a need to know. Promise me ...no one else can know. Marcie, I already made that promise.

**Marcie, sweet dreams my Love.
He blew her a kiss.**

She fell asleep thinking about "my Love".

Stephen headed back to Cliff walk for several hours to process everything. Each time he passed the "Center" he stopped in to check on the Boxman. Not good.

Chapter Twenty-One

Next day, Sunday. Crews could be seen moving the flat screens and speakers to outside lawn of Mercy Chapel facing Ochre Point Avenue. Everyone could figure that out. Sister had promised the Boxman she'd handle all his final affairs.

Monday morning. The Dean of Nursing, summons

Sister, Stephen, Dawn and Marcie to the "Center". They begin to pray.

Marcie is signing prayer.

No tears just Hope.

By the Grace of God, the Boxman crosses his...

"Final Threshold of Hope".

Joyful sorrow.

Stephen is in hallway now. Sends text message (to house staff), Forte dei Marmi, Italy reading: "Come now! Limousine will arrive in one hour. Bombardier Challenger 300 (Mach .82) at Pisa International Airport. Tail #.... Arrive T.S. Green airport, Warwick Rhode Island. Limousine awaits."

Received message. Packed and ready to go. Will see you at The Viking. He's (the blind man), eager to see you again.

A hearse arrives about an hour later. White Hood still draped upon him. Sister gets busy! She instructs the three to go down to America's Cup and place a sign on the boxes reading. "The Boxman has gone home to eternal rest. Visit Salve.edu/.... for more information." And...bring the plastic chair to me.

One hour later the web page read: "Our dear friend, the Boxman, has left us". Three days of mourning has already commenced. Tomorrow (Tuesday), visitors can call with final respects at Ochre Court, Ochre Point Avenue, Newport, 8:00

A.M. to 8:00 P.M.

A Requiem Mass (for the repose of a Soul) will commence at 9:00 A.M., Wednesday, Our Lady of Mercy Chapel, Campus of Salve Regina University. (By request of the Boxman), donations can be made to American School for the Deaf, West Hartford, Connecticut.

Tuesday, 7:00 A.M. The Boxman arrives Ochre Court. A flag draped, closed coffin, "rested" on the "Dance" floor. He was a Gulf War Veteran. There have been exhaustive studies concerning links to Parkinson's disease and brain tumors in Veterans of the Gulf War. Suspected causes include vaccinations, oil well fires, chemical and biological weapons, depleted uranium, Pyridostigmine Bromide (PB), (a drug to protect against the nerve agent Soman), pesticides, infectious diseases and other potential toxicities. The Boxman had been part of a number of these studies. He never complained about his diagnosis and the potential link to his service. He always referred to the Army as the "Great United States Army". He always said; you know... freedom is not free; a new installment comes due for each generation.

Ochre Point Avenue was again closed off. A procession of well-wishers commenced immediately at 8:00 A.M. and went till the last moment of calling hours. Sister, Dawn, Stephen, Marcie, the Yachtsman and the Boxman's brother represented the Boxman's family and were the receiving line all day. Many previously unknown stories of the Boxman were shared with them. All conveyed their deepest sympathies. That evening, University Security, surrounding Ochre Court, stood present the entire evening with lights flashing the whole night. Sister had already spoken with the persons the Boxman wished to be his pallbearers. All were moved.

Wednesday, 9:00 A.M. casket sits on raised platform floor in Mercy Chapel in front of altar. His wheelchair and "the" plastic chair sat facing each other. The "White Hood" draped over the wheelchair. Mass began as hundreds watched the screens outside in a cold strong wind. No one complained. Dawn was on the Altar signing everything to Marcie. Father's homily focused upon "Compassion". He reminded everyone what Compassion means, the willingness to suffer with another as the Boxman did.

Just before Communion, a multitude of students entered and surrounded the entire Chapel. Sister had arranged it all. Musicians took their places near the Altar. It was the University Chorus with their long-time choir master. They began to sing as they had several days ago, during their Christmas Concert at Ochre Court. As multiple Eucharistic Ministers distributed Communion, both inside and out, they sang The Hallelujah Chorus from Handel's Messiah. (Link filmed in Ochre Court on Marcie and Stephen's dance floor). Dawn stood firm and signed the entire thing. Marcie could "Feel" the music. Beautiful!

When Communion had ended, all sat quietly in prayer and reflection and gratitude. Only one violinist remained on the Altar. Father was sitting in his chair and all noticed him gesture to Stephen who rose. All eyes were upon him. He walked to the microphone and stood silently for some time. Dawn continued to sign. Friends he began, we are here to honor and say "goodbye" to our dear friend. With God's Grace, The Boxman reached out to save a wretch like me. I once was lost, but now am found, was blind but now I see. I have a final personal gift for Mark. He walked through a door to the right of the altar. Moments later he emerged holding a gentleman's hand. There was a gasp. Everyone knew this "Blind" man. And so, accompanied by the single violinist he sang...Con Te Partiro (Time to Say Goodbye). It was Andrea Bocelli. Dawn could not sign...she did not know Italian! Tears. Silence.

Stephen helped Andrea to a seat next to Sister. Sister rose to the microphone. Dear friends, we will now have Marcie give the Eulogy. She rose to the altar and stood alongside the casket. Dawn was to her side, verbally interpreting as Marcie signed. Marcie signed slowly adding to the importance of every word.

I have been greatly blessed to have known the Boxman. I've had many private conversations with him while he was here with us in Newport. I cherish every moment. I will never forget him. He was good to me. He accepted me just the way I am. He loved me. It's as if I've known him my entire life. Stephen looked on as did Sister.

They were the only others who knew!

(Remember this at the beginning of this story?)

*"Dawn interpreted for Sister. Marcie, you wrote in your college application essay that you wanted to be a "Compassionate" nurse and the first Deaf Nurse to graduate Salve. You'll accomplish both here, but especially, in the care of our most vulnerable patients. **Sister had no idea of the magnitude of what she had just said to Marcie!!!** For now, only two persons on earth knew that significance."*

Marcie turned to face Dawn more directly. Dawn continued to speak everything aloud. Dawn, you are my best friend! I love you! I have something I need to tell you. You are the reason I am here at Salve. You're my sister in every way. You know everything about me except, (long pause) … for one thing.

Silence.

You remember the other night; you said you were sorry that my Dad did not make the Ball? I said to you...but he did, you just missed him. That's true! You didn't recognize him. You haven't recognized him for several months already.

Dawn... (Another long pause)

Marcie started shaking. Her entire body was shaking.

Tears exploded from her eyes.

They cascaded down her cheeks.

She made no attempt to wipe them.

They fell to the floor. Dawn looked on in pity.

Dawn, only two people now know what I'm about to tell you. Only Sister, the Boxman and Stephen knew till now. They were sworn to secrecy. You wondered why there was no last name in his obituary?

Dawn... you knew the Boxman long before Salve. I knew you would not recognize him. He was so sick.

He loved you too, especially for what you did for me at Lauralton. You are his second daughter.

Dawn signs, Marcie... dear God.

Dawn...forgive me, but he wanted it this way. He just wanted to be with me, as long as possible. To do his "Work".

Tears, tears, tears. A river of tears.

Dawn...

The Boxman... is my Dad.

Oh, dear God.

Dawn grabbed hold of Marcie, both weeping bitterly.

Everyone rose in thunderous applause both inside and out.

It was time. Pallbearers donned white gloves. Marcie and Dawn were in the front of the casket, followed by Sister and Stephen and finally the Yachtsman (who delayed his trip home) and the Boxman's brother. They carried the Boxman to the door of Mercy Chapel. Father read the prayer of Commendation.

Merciful Lord

Turn toward us and listen to our prayers:

Open the gates of Paradise for your servant Mark

And help us who remain

To comfort one another with assurances of Faith

Until we all meet in Christ

and are with you and with our brother Mark for ever

Through Christ our Lord, Amen

The Pall was removed from the casket and Father sprinkled it with Holy Water. All looked on. The American Flag was again placed upon the casket. They carried the Boxman to the waiting hearse. Several vans marked Salve Regina followed to a small cemetery in Connecticut to his final resting place alongside his wife. He was carried to the grave by the pallbearers. They all placed their arms around each other. Father then prayed:

Oh God, by whose mercy, the faithful departed find rest, send your Holy Angel, to watch over this grave, through Christ our Lord. Amen.

The military honor guard then fired three volleys from their rifles. Before approaching Marcie, one of the guards stooped to pick up the shell casings and then handed them to her. Then, they removed the flag and with unbelievable reverence, folded it. One approached Marcie and before handing her the flag said:

The people of the United States thank you.

Each placed a flower on the casket. Marcie, Dawn and Stephen held hands as they approached.

Marcie signed...Good job Dad!

They all stopped for dinner on the way back to Newport. They arrived 8:00.

Sister said to the two girls...meet me in my office at 9:00 in the morning. All fell into a deep sleep.

Chapter Twenty-Two

Good morning girls! He's already three days in Paradise!

Marcie and Dawn, I need to share with you, final arrangements made by Mark for your futures. Dawn, he knew your parents struggled to pay your tuition as he did for Marcie. He was very concerned about both your future financial obligations. He called me one evening and asked me to meet him on America's Cup. He took some papers from an envelope. He said, Sister, I'm doing what I can regarding my two daughters' future here at Salve. This is a quit claim deed transferring ownership of my home in Connecticut to the University. Upon my passing, you can sell it and use the proceeds towards Marcie and Dawn's ongoing tuitions. I said to him, but where will Marcie go if your home was sold? Maybe she can stay with Dawn? He handed me the documents. I said to him, Mark, stay focused upon your "Work".

Let that be your only concern! I'll take care of the rest. As soon as I arrive back at my office, I will shred these documents.

I called Stephen to my office as we had already received help from his Dad. I asked Stephen if he would speak to his Dad. Two days later, a check arrived in our finance department with payment in full, for your next three years here at Salve. Yes, for both of you! Marcie, a new quit claim deed was drawn up and your home is now in your name. Mark has already personally thanked Stephen and his Dad. Just work on becoming Compassionate nurses!

The two girls left…stunned. They were headed to Miley when Marcie pointed to Stephen heading their way. They both took off running and threw their arms around him. He signed…what was that for? Oh Stephen, for what you and your Dad did for us. I'm just looking out for myself. How could

I have survived another three years here without both of you?

Things began to return to normal. It had been a complete whirlwind since the beginning of the semester. All were drained. Stephen began his studies in Education. He had a new vision as visionaries do.

Marcie and Dawn plunged into the rigors of Nursing. You needed a crane to lift some of the nursing textbooks. Not for the faint of heart. Stephen, Marcie and Dawn were inseparable. Always encouraging each other. Time passed. Stephen had a plan. Since he had changed majors from Criminal Justice to Education, he was now one semester behind Dawn and Marcie.

His new goal was to graduate with them. It absolutely had to be this way! He did the necessary calculations and increased his credit load to finish on time. He even took some summer courses back home. Marcie and Dawn were eventually consumed by the addition of clinical work. This meant rising and travelling to their clinical sites before most students awoke. Stephen would occasionally drive to where they were and treat them to lunch. It was not uncommon for them to return after the Miley cafeteria had closed. For obvious reasons, Marcie and Dawn were assigned the same clinical sites. As for Stephen and his affinity for ASL, his advisor arranged for "Study Abroad" at American School for the Deaf. He made countless trips from Newport to West Hartford, Ct. He'd leave early enough to make the ninety-mile, one-way trip, on days he did not have classes. He'd spend the entire school day there. He structured his class load to allow two free days per week for his "Work". His plan was to hone his ASL with one additional twist. Stephen's was a very keen mind. If he wasn't up to some new challenge, he was seemingly bored. He had to have a challenge on his plate. Something big. That something big, which he kept from even Marcie and Dawn, was to learn to read lips. This was huge. He had a "Professional" goal to understand that process. When he was with his mentor, he would fall back upon Katherine's training method. He would place ear plugs in his ears. Only then could he have some chance of acquiring that amazing and exhausting skill. Truthfully, he hadn't quite figured out how that would help him, as he was from the "Hearing" community but that didn't faze him. He imagined passing the skill forward to the Deaf. He continued his lessons with Dawn unabated. He quickly realized why classrooms for the Deaf were small and why the desks were arranged the way they were. Why the hallways were extra wide to accommodate persons signing. These things were intriguing to him. It was a facet of life he'd never known before. Things like this just captured his imagination and spurred him on. He had a special interest in the athletic program at ASD because of his background. He began to have "Secret Conversations" with someone. When summer arrived and he didn't have a summer course to attend, he'd spend his time at Camp Isola Bella (for the Deaf) in Twin Lakes (Salisbury) Connecticut which Marcie knew all about. He never had a better summer. Marcie and Dawn visited him regularly.

Freshman turned sophomore turned Junior.

Marcie's academic advisor had begun to meet with her and Dawn over a very important matter. That matter was where Marcie could find work after obtaining her BSN (Bachelor of Science Nursing). This was not a trivial matter. It was a very, very big matter. As you would expect, Marcie and Dawn shared all of this with Stephen. In typical fashion he began to run his "Game Tapes". Several weeks later, Stephen asked the girls to set up a meeting with their advisor and Sister to include him. They did. Stephen made a PowerPoint presentation. He began by saying... **"what if?"** All sat in amazement. The advisor said, Stephen... that could work! Why didn't we think of that? It all made sense. He had presented extensive data concerning video conferencing, i.e., VRI (Video Remote Interpreting), for the Deaf and hard of hearing in hospitals, especially Emergency Rooms. He made a sub presentation on dedicated high speed (Broadband) Internet connections with devoted exclusive bandwidth to support high definition video transmissions on both ends. Each endpoint supporting at least 1024 video calling, be uninterrupted and continuous, with an IP overhead of 1.2M Ethernet connection. They just looked at him. He dove in deeper. Next, he took them through a calculation.

23,700,000 X .0038 X .0073...That's 657!

There you have it! What if... just what if... those 657 patients and their doctors and nurses didn't need to be exclusively tied to bandwidth? Would there be better outcomes? Marcie jumped out of her seat and hugged him. She verbally yelled, Yes, Yes!

Is there any challenge that Stephen will not take on? You mention something to him, and he appears to have no reaction, and sometime later, he'll reveal a doctoral thesis. This time was no exception. Marcie signed "Wow" to him.

Their advisor said...I have work to do!

Stephen always had several doctoral theses in his brain. That's what he did. For all the plans he had ever committed to, there was always one that cycled through his brain, continuously. It began several months after he had a footprint embroidered on his face. This was the plan of all plans.

This was epic! This was his Keystone plan! A plan like no other!

Stephen had a great talent. No matter how many plans he had in his brain at any one time, he had a knack for being able to compartmentalize them. He could close the file drawer on one thesis and open another. The two would not overlap. This thesis was different. He couldn't keep it in its file drawer. Those neurons kept firing and popping out and he could not stop them. They were firing when he awoke and the last neurons firing at night. Like Tasmanian devils! He'd had almost three years invested now. However; this was the plan that had the most variables. This was big, even by Stephen's standards. He was still having those "Secret" conversations with "someone". This plan was secret only to himself. This had the potential to be his biggest failure. A failure of this magnitude would have lifetime implications. Not only for himself but others as well. The fact that he even considered the possibility of failure was new to him. This could be calamitous. Only time would tell.

The girls were deeply focused on the NCLEX-RN exam. Nursing is one line of study that can have an abrupt ending. Although you can take the National Council Licensure Examination several times…if you can't pass it, you're all done! Go on to another profession. It must be this way. Nurses bridge the gap between life and death. They must know what they're doing. Fortunately for Salve nursing students, the Pass Rate for first time test takers is around ninety percent. That's mild consolation to the students. This little exam occurs about 45 days after graduation. They were studying night and day.

Senior year was racing along. Clinicals, NCLEX preparations, ASD, lip-reading. Stephen's "Ultra-Grand Plan" was progressing as were his private conversations with that secret someone. Dawn had met a nice young man during first semester of senior year. She was spending more and more time with him. By default, Stephen was now spending more time with Marcie. Since he was 100% fluent in ASL, this worked well for them both. Even though Stephen had plenty of girlfriends during high school, he seemingly had lost interest while planning for the Governor's Ball. He didn't have time to think, let alone, about those things. Even after the Ball and the Boxman's passing, he seemed to have lost interest. He never mentioned any romance to either Dawn or Marcie. As for Marcie... she had never been kissed. Things were beginning to ramp up for graduation. Many more conversations took place between Marcie, her advisor and Stephen. He took over exclusively for Dawn as far as this matter was concerned but also in other matters as well.

It appeared that Stephen and Marcie were now a couple... but not so. That mattered for naught now! Neither Dawn nor Stephen knew, Marcie had fallen deeply in Love with someone!

Had Stephen known this...?

Often, it was just Marcie and Stephen alone. They

discussed their fears and hopes. Yes, Stephen also had fears! Marcie confided that soon she'd be in the "Hearing World", all alone, for the first time ever. A plan for Marcie's Nursing Profession, was beginning to come

together nicely. It would require extensive travel for Marcie in the Tri-State region, but she was excited beyond "Sign".

Here is the thesis that Stephen had presented in his PowerPoint. Marcie would be living in her parents' former home in Shelton Connecticut after graduation. Right in the New York Tri-State region. This region has the highest population of any geographical region in the world. 23,700,000 people. Next, Stephen had calculated, that at .38% of the population there should be 90,060 Deaf or hearing-impaired persons in this region. Since .73% of the U.S. population will be admitted to a hospital per year, this meant that 657 or so Deaf or hearing-impaired persons should be admitted to hospitals in the Tri-State Region per year. His conclusion was that Marcie could be the main point of contact for these Deaf patients. She would be the primary contact during admissions, continuing care and discharge.

There could not possibly be a better situation for these patients. A BSN doing the interpretation! Marcie would personally visit as many as possible during admission and be an integral part of their care. Why was this so important? As was common knowledge amongst medical personnel, there could be significant challenges with VRI, video remote interpreting. These interpreters did not necessarily possess a strong medical background. Certainly, all did their best, but medical issues were not always precisely interpreted. This has always been a significant challenge. If Marcie could be the main point of contact, there would be an exponential increase in the interpreting process which doctors and nurses could rely upon in the treatment of Deaf patients. Marcie could evaluate their medical needs in person, as often as humanly possible, and input that information into the patient portal. In addition, she could personally convey the prescribed medical care plan to patients, answer questions, etc. She would be a travelling nurse! Doctors and nurses could text her with questions and their need for her to communicate directly with patients. What could be better for these Deaf patients? Marcie realized the significance of such an arrangement. She would be on call 24/7/365 but this did not faze her. This would be a nursing career like no other. She couldn't be happier about her future! It's not that VRI would not continue to be used but that Marcie would be the preferred first line of contact for medical interpretation for patients communicating in ASL. This would be especially true for planned admissions where Marcie's presence could be locked in beforehand. In fact, hospitals have been tasked with the requirement of providing on-site interpretation services by either locally sourced inter-preters or medically trained hospital employees knowing ASL. Having said that, it is a common reality that many medical environments fall far short of that directive. Conversely, some medical facilities have erroneously concluded that VRI satisfied all mandates regarding interpretation services for those using ASL. Unfortunately, those institutions which have relied exclusively on VRI have seen themselves tainted by poor outcomes (communication), resulting in numerous law-suits. Now, a licensed BSN-RN would do the inter-preting for as many Deaf patients as possible. She would personally perform vitals during any per-sonal patient contact and precisely convey that to the patient. She welcomed every possibility of as-sisting during childbirth as this is a time of crit-ical care and presents the need for immediate and accurate interpreting. She could immediately type the patients' condition, needs, etc., for the doctor or nurse to read. This could be a life saver for mother and child. Off-site she would have dir-ect remote access to any hospital's patient portal allowing immediate entry of interpreted patient data. Doctors and nurses would have immediate access to all interpreted data. Therefore, Stephen ended his Power Point with the following ques-tion. Would there be better outcomes? Yes, yes!

Marcie's advisor, the Dean of Nursing, was work-ing non-stop to put this all-in place. Many hospitals had already come onboard.

In addition to the purely moral incentive, to provide as real-time and medically accurate translation of ASL as possible, these hospitals could not ignore the potential for litigation should they fall short of regulations. This was all falling into place as outlined by Stephen. His thesis had determined that interpretation requirements for those using ASL is a highly fluid situation and not necessarily understood by many medical providers. A future association with Marcie, providing medically accurate, on-site translation, would have significant implications. As a rule of thumb, providers have approximately 18 minutes from the time of arrival of a patient using ASL to have VRI brought to their room, set up and an interpreter on the screen! There is no question that even with Marcie's contracted services that other modes of interpretation and VRI would remain important tools. Marcie would "bolster", all that may already be in place, by providing on-site and medically accurate interpretation as often as humanly possible.

Dawn was diligently exploring her own future. She had a keen interest in pediatric oncology. She was highly focused on specific hospitals especially Yale Children's Hospital. She also realized her mastery of ASL could be a Godsend to Deaf pediatric patients. She could still live at home and commute until she felt the need for her own place. Her parents were happy for her homecoming. They had greatly missed her. Marcie however would return to an empty home each day. Thanks to Stephen's Dad, both girls would go into the world with no student debt and this created opportunities for them both.

Chapter Twenty-Three

Stephen, Marcie and Dawn we're beginning to look down a road which left Salve. Their time together, their life together, was ending. This was weighing heavily upon them all. Very heavily. Truth be told, they were hurting in real and significant ways. None wanted to admit to it, so as not to drag the others down, but they all felt it and knew that the others felt it as well. Marcie and Dawn, the conjoined twins, having not been separated, were about to go in separate ways. But...Stephen made three. There has never been a documented case of conjoined triplets. However, these conjoined triplets were intricately connected in their hearts and spirits.

Even with today's technology, these conjoined triplets...

could not be separated!

They were triplets, in everything, for the past 4 years, and, for Dawn and Marcie, almost eight. Their four-year odyssey could not have occurred if even one had not been part. Lately, they were looking at each other in a manner of intense endearment. They were meek and lowly in heart. Many students looked forward to graduation and beginning a new chapter in their lives and rightfully so. But for these three, they were feeling intense pangs of separation. They were nervous about crossing the next Threshold of Hope. In a sense, they were somehow leaving their companions behind. Stephen was weighed down by these thoughts.

He had executed a search of the quantum computer in his head. He found and consumed a song non-stop.

He went to see Father. Stephen was humble in manner and spirit, free from pride, as he explained his Ultra-Grand Plan and his secret conversations. Father did however sense Stephen's fears that, both matters may not turn out well. Stephen, pray about these things. The outcomes are beyond your control. Stephen, God knows you are weary and burdened, but he says to you... "Come to me all who are weary and burdened and I will give you rest". Stephen, God already knows the outcomes of your humble plans. Be at Peace about these things, you have done all you can.

One thing was becoming increasingly clear. As luck would have it, all three would be geographically close to each other after graduation. Dawn would return home to Stratford, CT., and Marcie to Shelton Ct., to her parents' home. Unbe-

PETER RUSATSKY

knownst to the girls, Stephen had three job inter-
views all for the same position. The girls were in
Miley for lunch one afternoon and they spotted
Stephen running full speed toward the cafeteria.
Dawn had pointed to Marcie, "look". He was coming down Ochre Point Avenue. He jumped over
all the exterior stairs at Miley (the same ones he
smashed his face on) and flew into the cafeteria.
He was completely out of breath. He was on one
knee in front of both girls signing, "I did it!",
"I did it!" What Stephen...what? They hired me,
they hired me. Who? The American School for the
Deaf! I start in the fall!!! They all just hugged each
other...for a long time.

Stephen, where will you live? Maybe somewhere
near you guys? Maybe halfway between you and
ASD. Who knows? I'll be working at Camp Isola
Bella all summer, so I guess I'll have to decide by
graduation. Maybe...I'll...

Presently, only Father knew. Time was drawing
near to initiate his most audacious plan yet.
Others would have to know. First and foremost,
Sister. He asked her to meet him at Mercy Chapel.
They spoke for an hour. Stephen, I'll take care of
everything. Stephen, I'll second what Father said
to you. Pray over this and be accepting of the possibility this may not go as planned. Is your Father
on board with the other matter? He's putting
a plan together for himself. He's had two inter-
views. I'll talk to Dawn.

Behind McAuley, a great tent was being erected for graduation. Huge! Overlooking the ocean. Those two flat screens were also positioned to each side of the stage. Time was drawing close. One evening Stephen asked Dawn to meet him in "Their" study room in McKillop Library. Dawn, I need your help. I haven't found a place to live yet. Here's my plan...

What do you think?

Oh, Stephen, I'm in, God bless you!!!

Students and faculty wondered why another huge tent was being erected outside Ochre Court on the "Upper" lawn area. Across the top of the tent in massive letters..., "I have a dream!" That hadn't happened before. Sister took care of a request from Stephen. Every ticket for graduation had a special letter attached to it reading, "A benefactor is sponsoring a celebration following Commencement. All are invited. Food and drink for everyone. Beginning one hour after graduation till 9:00 P.M. Please join us".

Stephen still had a large chunk of money that was left over from the funds he had requested from his Dad. He figured no sense in not spending it. Dad had never asked for an accounting. He planned to put it to good use. Dawn don't forget about Vermont! I'll give you the address. Sister wants to go with you to get that other item. Let me know how much. I think I'm all set with the caterers. Brass Attack will be there. Grand piano...done.

Stephen was asked by both Dawn and Marcie to attend the Nursing Department's, "Blessing of the Hands" ceremony for graduating nurses. It had a tremendous impact on him. He never imagined such a thing. Now, the two women he loved the most, were going out into the world with sacred hands. He was deeply moved.

Chapter Twenty-Four

Friday, before graduation, Stephen goes nuts. He appeared in Miley around noon as Dawn and Marcie were eating. Truthfully, he'd gone nuts. His plan was complete, except for the distinct possibility it could be a catastrophic failure. I guess he thought he'd celebrate now, just in case. He had his smart phone playing a certain song over and over. Everyone could hear it. This song represented everything about his four years at Salve. He searched long and hard for it. As if he'd written the words himself. He was emotionally charged. He started dancing with every girl. Like a crazy person. Just grabbed their hands and danced throughout the cafeteria. It was, "The Simple Things are Free", by Jim Brickman and Rebecca Lynn Howard. About 15 seconds per girl. He was in his own world. Everyone liked Stephen so they jumped at the chance to dance with him. This was his grand finale or was it? When he was done, he danced himself right out of Miley and down Ochre Point

Avenue. This little celebration came at a cost to one girl. He danced with Dawn but forgot Marcie. She was hurt but realized he'd forgotten in all the excitement. She had not danced with him since the Governor's Ball. Oh well!

Yes...Every tear comes to dry!

Saturday, Hooding Ceremony and Baccalaureate Mass. Several thousand. Everyone had family except Marcie. With her tickets, she asked certain faculty members from ASD to attend. They were overjoyed!

Graduation Day!

Catering trucks were coming and going from the Ochre Court tent. This did not interfere with the Commencement in any way. People were arriving by the thousands. Perfect sunny day, a little ocean breeze. A slice of heaven to be in such a magnificent tent overlooking the Atlantic. Graduates assembled in Rogers Recreation Center. Stephen was fidgety. Marcie had asked Stephen, just three days ago, where he would be living. Don't know yet! Dawn and Stephen's parents were all there. The academic procession from Rogers Recreation Center began at 9:15 and Commencement Ceremony began at 10:00. It would last till noon. Stephen knew this. He had to know this.

The Commencement speaker was the Yachtsman. He spoke about global responsibility. He chal-

lenged all to be globally ecologically responsible. A challenge was issued to clean up the
world's oceans! He spoke about the North Atlantic Garbage Patch. Hundreds of kilometers across,
containing man-made debris with a density of
200,000 pieces of debris per square kilometer. He
pointed to the ocean and said, "Its right out there".
Salve's Yacht can reach it, linger, and return on a
single tank. Its range is 6000 nautical miles and
carries 30,000 gallons of fuel. Go there, do something! That garbage will be on "this shore" soon.
The ocean's garbage has already devastated shore-
lines around the world. I've seen this with my own
eyes. This is not just a challenge for Salve's new
Oceanographic Department but for everyone that
has eyes that see, and ears that hear. This world is
counting on you. All were moved, inspired.

The ceremony was nearly over. Marcie wondered
why the flat screens were never on. Maybe a technical problem? Sister came to the microphone.
She thanked the Yachtsman and reinforced his
plea.

Dear friends, I was approached by one of your
classmates who asked if he could say a few words.
He needs no introduction. I will miss this young
man. Salve is different because of him. He chal-
lenged himself and this entire University to be
more Compassionate, more Hopeful, more Merciful and more Loving. You all know him and I'm
sure you know of whom I speak.

His personal journey was long and difficult. He

never wavered from becoming a better person. He's a living testament to perseverance. I must say, he has been an inspiration to me these past four years. He has accepted a teaching position at the American School for the Deaf in West Hartford, Connecticut. Salve sends him forth to continue his good works. Dawn had signed all of Sister's introduction to Marcie. Dawn and Marcie were now on the edges of their seats. He rose and every eye was upon him, including his parents.

Stephen had nothing in his hands. Only a wireless microphone headset mic. When he reached the podium, there was dead silence. The flat screens suddenly awoke. He stood there for a good thirty seconds not

saying anything. He "Crossed" himself and "Signed" everything for Marcie as he spoke.

First let me say...I am a new person because of this University. I had the privilege of knowing, the two women... I love the most... in this entire world. They rescued a lost sheep. They fed and nurtured me. Thank-you Sister, Katherine, Bill, Father, and all of you who came to my rescue. Thanks Mom and Dad.

He was trembling and his voice was cracking.

It was time!!!

Marcie..., you've been asking me where I'll be living. Each time I've said, "I don't know". I still do not know. I also heard from Dawn, that you were hurt, that I didn't dance with you the other day.

Marcie, (long pause), I'd apologize… but… it was intentional. Everyone was transfixed on him. On one screen was Stephen and a cameraman filming Marcie for the other. Her face took up most of that screen. He tried to compose himself.

When we danced at the Ball it was
the highlight of my life.
I promised myself that I would not…, I would not…
dance with you again, until…
until, we were…married!

Marcie was now trembling. All eyes were upon her. Dawn was holding both her hands. Sister had made sure that Marcie had an aisle seat and Dawn was next to her. I need to tell you something else. When we leave here today, I'm hoping you'll be my wife. I want to have supper made for you every night, and since I don't have anywhere to live…

I'm hoping to spend the rest
of my life with you!
Marcie signed nothing in return.
Tears exploded out of her eyes.
She made no attempt to wipe them.
A River of Tears cascaded down her cheeks
and silently fell from her chin.
They found peaceful rest upon
her and Dawn's hands.

Stephen left the podium and proceeded towards her. A river of tears continued flowing from her eyes. He knelt, and in perfect sign said...

Marcie will you marry me?

She stared into his eyes, and... shook her head yes. He continued to sign...Marcie, will you marry me today? Father is waiting for us in the Chapel. Dawn and Sister picked out your wedding dress. We even have a Marriage License but don't ask me how!

He took her hands from Dawn and held them tightly. Now the tears fell upon their hands. She stared into his eyes. She had never signed a word. Till now! Stephen's microphone picked up what Marcie replied for all to hear!

With great emotion, Marcie spoke "aloud" ..., Stephen, I've been in Love with you for three years now!

She lip read..., Marcie...will you marry me today? Will you be my Keystone? She shook her head yes! He took a ring from his pocket and placed it on her finger.

He kissed her on the cheek with deep affection. Meet me in Mercy Chapel in ten minutes. Everything is ready!

Chapter Twenty-Five

Stephen rose and signed, "got to go" and took off running towards Mercy Chapel. Dawn took a

Kleenex and tenderly wiped Marcie's face. Marcie signed to Dawn... did you know? Yes, Marcie I did. Stephen couldn't keep his love for you to himself! They took off running. Thunderous applause and screaming. No one left their seats. They knew they'd be watching the wedding on the flat screens. The letter that accompanied the tickets had also said, if there is a red dot on your ticket, leave for Mercy Chapel immediately after Commencement. Now they knew why.

About one hundred specially invited guests immediately left for the Chapel and were quickly seated. In a small room, Sister and Dawn dressed Marcie in her wedding dress and fixed her hair and makeup. Stephen had not seen the dress. Ten minutes on the dot, Marcie and Dawn stood at the entrance of the Chapel. Dawn would give her away. Just before they proceeded down the aisle, a message began to play over the speakers. Stephen and Father were waiting at the altar. Stephen in tuxedo.

Dawn knew about this and signed to Marcie.

It began...Marcie; this is from your Father. A few weeks before the Ball, Stephen told me about his dream to marry you around graduation.

He knew our conversations were coming to an end. He was beyond happy to share that with me. He knew your Mother had passed. He mentioned his hope of finding your Father, without your knowing, to ask him for your hand in Marriage. As you know, the two of us had many private talks. I came to love him as a son. I knew I wouldn't make this day. I had to tell him. I said to him...Stephen, ask me now! You can imagine his reaction. That is how he found out. I asked him to record this message on his "fancy" phone. He constantly, constantly talked about you and how he had fallen in Love. I could not have imagined a better husband for you. He is a good man. I was thrilled to say yes. We hugged. I needed that Peace before joining your Mother. We love you both. Mom and I will be watching!

Pachelbel's Canon in D played. The girls processed down the aisle. No words were said when Dawn placed Marcie's hands in Stephen's. When they were coupled, Dawn held their hands together in hers and bent down to kiss their hands. She then left for the side of the Altar where she would sign the entire Mass to Marcie. The altar had two vases holding the most amazing Daylilies anyone had ever seen.

They took their place at the kneelers continuing to hold hands. Hundreds and hundreds and hundreds, were watching in the tent. When the moment arrived, Father read the vows. Dawn was to Father's side so Marcie could read her sign.

He began, Stephen do you take Marcie, to be your lawfully wedded wife, to have and to hold, from this day forward, for better, for worse, for richer, for poorer, in sickness and in health, until death do you part?

He said and signed, "I do".

Marcie, do you take Stephen to be your lawfully wedded husband, to have and to hold, from this day forward, for better, for worse, for richer, for poorer, in sickness and in health, until death do you part.

She signed and said, "I do"

What God has joined let no man put asunder.

Dawn, may I have the rings?

Father blessed them. They exchanged the rings with promises of unconditional love and fidelity. By the power vested in me…

I now pronounce you man and wife.

Stephen, you told me that you have never so much as kissed this woman who is now your wife. Here's your chance!

You may kiss the bride! And they kissed.

You could hear the crowd erupt outside.

About 30 minutes or so later, Mass was concluding. Father said, I now present Mr. and Mrs.…., at that very moment, the great 1910 bells cast by Meneely Bell Company erupted in the Bell Tower. Wow!

Let the party begin! All the guests, a thousand or so who were able to attend, were immediately directed to the tent behind Ochre Court. Michael spent every cent of his Father's funds. Incredibly beautiful. Flowers everywhere. In each arrangement were several Daylilies of the same type. The same ones as on the Altar. Marcie had no idea of the profound significance of those Daylilies. She'd know soon! Everyone commented on them including Marcie. Brass Attack, alive and well!

First dance! A gentleman took his seat at the grand piano, played and sang Van Morrison's, "Have I told you lately that I love you".

> *Cheek to cheek.*
> *No more tears.*
> *Every tear had come to dry.*
> *Joy!*

It was now 2:00. Six hours till sunset!

You name it, Stephen arranged for it. His parents were proud beyond belief. They had not known anything. All night long they said, "We're Stephen's parents". The day flew by for the new couple. They never actually sat down. Having graciously made the rounds, meeting everyone and dancing and dancing. They ate while standing. The dance floor was packed constantly. Katherine and Professor McBride (Bill) finally found the time to be together. Stephen had one interesting brainstorm when planning their wedding. He surmised that people might have wanted to give them a wedding present, except that, no one had any idea they were going to a wedding that day. To one side of the tent were several tables. The banner above them read "Make a donation to the American School for the Deaf in honor of Stephen and Marcie". The line was never ending. They processed

credit cards all day. Final tally, six figures. Amen.
Stephen began to watch the time obsessively. He
had a private conversation with Dawn. Is everything there? Yes, I took it there personally. Even
the bunny pajamas? Yes. Did she notice anything?
No, after she packed up, I went through her boxes.
She didn't notice anything! Great! He knew he
wouldn't be seeing Dawn for a while. He drew her
to himself and hugged her for a long while, rock-
ing back as forth. Not saying a word. He removed a
box from his pocket. He asked her to hold it while
he opened it.

He removed the most beautiful diamond
necklace and...
placed it upon her.

He found his parents. Thanks Mom and Dad, I love
you both. We're leaving soon. I'll call you.
Sister, I love you. Hugging her, he whispered in her
ear... thanks for everything and may God protect
and keep you. I'll see you soon. You are my hero!

Sunset 8:01

Time was drawing near. Stephen owed Marcie a
dance! Dawn and Marcie were off in a corner but
under the gaze of everyone. Marcie, this is from
Stephen and handed her a beautifully wrapped
box with a fresh Daylily on it. After opening it, she
said to Dawn...what's this? It's called a "Wireless
Ecosystem". It's his Wedding gift to you. Eyes were

riveted as Marcie put it on over her wedding dress. It was now available commercially since his training with a prototype.

The party was in full swing. Lots of alcohol had been consumed. Stephen made his way to the microphone. The band paused. It was now 7:55. He signed to Marcie and spoke aloud to everyone. Thank-you, thank-you! Marcie and I love you all. As he was speaking, workers were taking all the sides off the tent. Rather hastily. He addressed Marcie who was still with Dawn. Marcie, I believe I owe you a dance. The pianist took his seat again at the grand piano. Remember I told you, I had purposely not danced with you on Friday at Miley. We'll I'd like that dance now...with my wife! To the same song! Rebecca Lynn Howard appeared with a microphone standing next to the piano. All the lights were turned off except one, on the couple. Stephen led her to the dance floor and everyone surrounded them. Time 7:57. Sunset in four minutes.

He turned it on!

And so, began the "Simple things".
(Watch for two children with "Boxes" on their heads!)

*A thousand chiming church bells ring,
the simple things are free.*

All Marcie could sign was…Stephen, Oh my God!

His hand lovingly on her head as it rested on his shoulder. A single, "follow-spot", illuminating "their" dance. About thirty seconds from the end, the tent became illuminated from outside. A circular pattern revolved around the tent ceiling. It circled several times. Their dance ended with a tender kiss. What the heck was happening? Stephen knew! He took Marcie by the hand and ran outside. Everyone running behind. With the sound of the music, people hadn't heard the noise till now. Hovering just off the Cliff Walk, above the Ocean, was that luxury Sikorsky S-76C helicopter. Another "follow-spot", was illuminating its side as it just hovered there.

Its side read… "I love you Marcie!".

Stephen had made sure there was enough room for its landing between the tent and Cliff walk on the lower level of the Great Lawn of Ochre Court. People were stunned. The tent sides were removed to help with the rotor wash. It began to inch its way to the landing site. No one could believe this! The wind was furious. It gently touched down. Stephen signed to Marcie…ready?

**Yes! Yes!
This time we're going together!**

They walked under the intense rotor wash. Blades whirling at nearly full speed. Near the door, Stephen turned Marcie towards the crowd.

He "dipped" her, for all to see, as he kissed her.

Hair and dress flying everywhere. They entered, the door closed, and they could both be seen waving in the windows. The rotor went to full speed. The tent was fluttering wildly. Everyone was waving and screaming. It began to lift off. It made a slow turn over the water, the "follow- spot" still on it.

When the other side became visible it read...,

"Thanks Salve!"

It continued around till it was facing everyone. The pilot "dipped" its nose three times in a final farewell.

It banked steeply and set off into the darkness. OMG!

"The Ocean and the sky...the way we feel tonight."

Marcie, this thing flies at 178 mph. Where are we going? Can't tell you, other than about 130 air miles from here. We'll be there in 45 minutes.
A small town in Southern Vermont was ground zero. GPS coordinates were locked in. On approach, Marcie was glued to the window. From several hundred feet above, she could see a tree

house. It was all lit up. They were in South New-fane, Vermont at the Treehouse Village Inn. The Inn had spray painted a landing zone per Stephen's precise instructions. The same spotlight that illuminated the tent was now shining down on the landing zone. The pilot gingerly coaxed the bird to a landing alongside the pond. Blades still whirling, Stephen said, Marcie, wait here. He exited the door and she could see him run up the stairs of the tree house. A moment later, he was back with a sweater size box wrapped in wedding paper with a beautiful bow. Put this on, I'll be just outside. Several minutes later she appeared at the door of the helicopter. She had on the bunny pajamas, complete with hood and ears. He signed to her...

ever since I tucked you in, I longed for this moment.

He took her in his arms and carried her up to the treehouse. They waved from the porch as their "transportation" disappeared.

Chapter Twenty-Six

Springtime in Vermont! Glorious! Holding hands every minute of every day, they wasted no time exploring all there was to see and do. Stephen had also arranged for two mountain bikes and a car with bike rack. They would be there for six days. Where didn't they go? Rafting down the Rock River and West River into Brattleboro,

Mount Snow mountain biking, Brattleboro shopping and wonderful restaurants, a picnic at Townshend Dam, rock climbing, Grafton Cheese, paddle boarding on Sunset Lake. Wilmington Vermont, with its fine shops and the Anchor Restaurant. They were enthralled with the Peace they found here.

They'd ride their bikes every evening in both directions on Dover Road. One evening, the Inn packed them a picnic dinner. They found the Williamsville Covered Bridge, 1.6 miles from Treehouse Village Inn. Lots of selfies. They continued to the West Dummerston Covered Bridge on Route 30. Someone offered to take their picture. Several miles later, they came to the largest bridge in Vermont. "Dubbed the Bridge to Nature" a balanced cantilever bridge, part of I-91. 1,036 feet in length and 100 feet above the West River. Marcie, that cost sixty million! The planners of this amazing bridge created a small park beneath it, complete with picnic tables. It is staggering to look up at it. They had a beautiful picnic that evening, watching the West River pass by, forming a small lake, just downstream in Brattleboro, opposite Grafton Village Cheese.

One morning Stephen said to her... after breakfast, I have a huge surprise for you. What Stephen? It's a surprise! It's so close we can walk there. Only about a mile. They arrived, hand in hand, only twenty minutes later. Marcie read the sign, "Olallie Daylily Farm", on Auger Hole Road.

Marcie couldn't believe her eyes. 2,500 cultivars, the "Extra Early" varieties, just blooming. They walked through the rows in utter amazement. Stephen, this is a wonderful surprise. Marcie, that's only part of the surprise. Olallie was always producing new cultivars. He suddenly stopped and said, "Here's your surprise!" She looked around but was confused. Stephen? Look down Marcie! Stephen, these are the ones from our wedding! Yes, Marcie but look closer. Then she saw it. Stephen had arranged to have one of their newest cultivars named after her. The small sign read...

"Olallie Marcie's Bloom".
(Here is the actual Daylilly!)
OMG Stephen.
I love you!

They did not miss hiking up Oregon Mountain and Harris Hill Ski Jump. Visited Brattleboro Museum and Art Center. In the evenings, from their lawn chairs, they were especially amused by watching the Ruby-Throated Hummingbirds visiting the nectar feeder. They learned they are the only species of Hummingbird to visit Vermont and that they arrive and depart Vermont with phenomenal precision. One evening, in the Inn lobby, they came upon a small book called Vermont 251 Club. They promised each other that they would someday join that Club by visiting all 251 towns and cities in Vermont. You can also purchase a Vermont 251 Club journal to memorialize your journeys. Stephen had already obtained one online so he could journal the towns they visited on their Honeymoon.

One thing they had to wait for till Thursday. Although they had already visited several wonderful restaurants, the Innkeepers mentioned that there was one restaurant they could not miss. They are only open Thursday through Sunday evenings. Stephen was not about to take her the Sunday they arrived. That would mean giving up the Bunny Pajamas. Those pajamas and all the clothing she would need that week, were pilfered from Marcie's packed dorm boxes by Dawn. She drove them personally, all the way to Vermont and the Inn. Anyways, they had better things to do that evening. The Inn had provided a platter of Vermont (Grafton Village) cheese, a Charcuterie Board, (everything Vermont), and beautiful Vermont fruits, flowers, Champagne and Vermont "Long Trail Double Bag" beer. Stephen asked the Innkeeper, who prepared this wonderful food? She said, the same place you're going Thursday evening. The Williamsville Eatery, just down the road. You passed it on your bike ride the other night.

When the innkeeper made their reservations, Laurie, Glen, Dillon and Sarah, all knew they were Newlyweds. A bottle of Champagne awaited them. They couldn't help but notice the chalk board that listed all their local and regional suppliers. Really farm to table. In keeping with tradition, Dillon had foraged that day for an unusual ingredient for dessert. When Marcie saw it on the menu, she gestured for Laurie to come to her. Stephen interpreted. What is this Japanese Knotweed? Well, it's one of the world's most invasive plants. Hurricane Irene did an excellent job of spreading it everywhere. I'm sure you've seen it. About eight feet tall and looks like bamboo. We saw it! We thought it was bamboo! Well, we're doing our part in eradication, by turning it into a dessert. We'll have two!

Wow! They had the best meal of their lives. Laurie, Stephen said, we have only one night remaining, tomorrow. Would you have a table for us? Stephen, please pick the table and the time. We'll do anything for our Newlyweds. Will you still have the Knotweed? Yes!

The secret discussions! Friday, Stephen rose early and went for a walk alone. Marcie was sound asleep. He decided to call his Father. Dad, its Stephen. Stephen how are you and Marcie? Mom and I have been praying for both of you all week. I asked the pilot where he took you. He told me Vermont. Wonderful choice. We are so happy. Dad, we're great! We've done more than humanly possible this week. I think we've Max-Q'd. His Dad, an engineer understood that. Marcie is still sleeping. We only have dinner plans tonight so she can sleep all day if she wishes. I've got to tell you about the Williamsville Eatery when we get home. You and Mom would love it.

Dad, how are the other things going? Stephen, I've taken stock of my life and myself, everything is sold!

The helicopter too? Yes, delivered to new owner yesterday. Just had to have the sides re-painted. Thanks Dad, I knew you wouldn't be upset about that. Was lucky to get 6.5 Mil for it. You'll miss that helicopter, won't you Dad? Honestly Stephen, you and I are off to bigger and way better things.

Dad, is your company sold? Transaction all complete. Dad, I'm proud of you! Your entire life was devoted to that medical device company. Yes Stephen, but too much of my life. We helped save and extend the lives of many people. It's time for younger ones to take over. I'm embarrassed to realize how much time I lost with you. Dad forget about it. We're good, always have been. So, is everything ready to go? Everything! Remember Dad, this time, it's only for fun. I know Stephen, and I promise, it will always remain that way. Thanks, Dad. I love you! Not a word to anyone except Mom of course. Bye Dad. Bye Stephen. Tell Marcie... Mom and I love her. Will do.

Chapter Twenty-Seven

"Every day's a brand-new sky"

Marcie and Dawn passed the NCLEX exam with

flying colors. Relief. Marcie and Stephen moved into her old home. Stephen was amazed at how the Boxman cared for his home being so sick. Everything was meticulous. Nothing needed caring for. It was finished just before he left. He had done this for Marcie, not knowing her future with Stephen. When he did know of Stephen's plans, he shipped a wedding gift there and called a neighbor to retrieve it and hold it for the next three years. They delivered it to the Newlyweds upon their arrival. The couple was deeply, deeply moved by the Boxman's planning! The day he left, by medical transport van to Newport, he sat and thought of his wife, Marcie and their lives together in this home. He realized he'd not be returning here. He raised his hand as a blessing and prayed that God would bless Marcie when she returned. All of this would have been for naught if Sister had not shredded that quit claim deed. Inside the box was a period antique pendulum clock. A simple note read...,

*"Cherish every second of your lives together,
Love, Mom and Dad"*

Marcie began her new job. What a blessing to the Deaf community. One of her first experiences was assisting a Deaf Mom through delivery. Just beautiful! It was working out as planned. Her skills were immediately in demand. Hospitals which contracted for her help could not imagine how they managed without someone like her. Marcie, for her part, was "beyond words". As a younger person, she had wondered and worried about her future. This was beyond anything she could ever have imagined. Fulfilling, beyond her dreams. She was establishing many friends including Doctors and Nurses, especially Hospitalists. When these hospitals became aware of a Deaf admission, they now looked forward to all they could offer that Soul. Compassion, mercy, hope, and love. Beautiful!

Stephen immediately began his summer position at Camp Isola Bella. It was a little bit of a ride, about 1 hour 20 minutes from Shelton, Ct. to Salisbury Ct., but wound through some of the state's most picturesque scenery in the northwest hills. He never felt it was a long journey. He just loved it! And, they loved him. All these "Campers" would already know him when school began. That would be a great plus. One of the newer challenges presented to him were the various ways the deaf campers communicated. With Marcie and Dawn, it was always ASL. Now it was ASL, oral, aural, lip-reading or some mixture. Of course, he was up for this and amazed by it all. He had the deepest respect for everyone. Surprise turned to amazement as he discovered the enormous number of activities available to all. He especially enjoyed, "Family Day", and the opportunity to meet parents and siblings. Stephen couldn't count the number of times parents would say or sign...Mr. Burns, we've heard all about you. Everyone loves you. We are so happy we have you! Thank-you. The children call me Stephen so you as well. "Mr." makes me feel old. Seems like just yesterday I was their age. Stephen didn't want the summer to end. He reminisced about his own childhood. What he remembered was the intense pressure to excel in sports. He had promised himself he'd never do that to any child. He was about "fun", and all the campers benefited from that. Stephen was the pied piper. Although the entire staff was simply wonderful, campers clamored to be with him. There was just something about Stephen.

He tried his best to fulfill one of the promises he had made to Marcie. That was to cook her dinner every chance he got. He of course considered grocery shopping part of that commitment. Nearly every evening, he greeted her with a hug and kiss, and they enjoyed each other's company over a lengthy dinner. They never, ever tired of "hearing" about each other's day. They relished it. Dishes? Why yes...that was part of Stephen's commitment. Stephen had the benefit of eating all his meals with the campers, but Marcie missed many of hers without the slightest of concerns. They were in love and enjoying every minute of life itself.

Dawn began her position at Yale New Haven Children's Hospital in pediatric oncology. This specialty had been on her radar since sophomore year. She had many conversations with Sister and Father as to this special calling. She was acutely aware of the joys and heartaches this profession would comprise. She would stay focused on the joy of being a medical partner, in care of the most vulnerable. Just what Salve prescribed! Dawn realized it would never be possible to isolate herself to only the medical aspects of this profession. It would require utmost attention to mercy, compassion, hope and love for her patients and their families. Salve's doctrine had surely prepared her well. She loved her work and couldn't have imagined a more rewarding profession.

All three got together as often as possible which was frequently. Dawn was often invited to dinner where ASL flowed like fine wine. This was a new chapter in their lives together. The triplets were back together. Who knew that Dawn and Marcie's meeting at Lauralton Hall would have led to this? It was not lost on any of them. Marcie and Dawn would visit Stephen at camp, sometimes together but sometimes alone depending on their schedules.

The Secret Conversation!

What time? Noon! Lunch! Marcie and I will come together. It was Stephen's first week at American School for the Deaf. He simply loved it. How could life have ever turned out this way? When the girls arrived, Marcie asked Dawn to drive around the complex of her old school, and she pointed out everything to her. Dawn was amazed by the size of ASD. She had been there a number of times with

Marcie but never had time for the complete tour. Marcie made sure to show her the memorials to Thomas Hopkins Gallaudet, Alice Coggswell and Laurent Clerk, the founders of ASD. Dawn was very moved and emotional. They entered the main entrance and Marcie was recognized by all! Many hugs. Hello Mrs. Burns! They all knew the girls were coming for lunch with Stephen.

God works in many mysterious ways!
Too many... once in a million occurrences...
to be purely coincidence.

Stephen had been working on his final plan for some time now. The "secret" plan. It involved not a single helper, as was not the case, in all his previous "endeavors". Truth be told, no one knew during its entirety. Not a single person including Marcie. Eventually only a handful at ASD would come to know. Stephen held on to this dream in total secrecy. It had to be that way. The plan was a culmination of a personal dream and personal hope. A gift of sorts to himself and the "Secret Someone". In Stephen's mind this was the culmination of his journey, largely based on Forgiveness and Mercy. He had received Forgiveness and Mercy and now it was his turn to pay it forward. Stephen met the girls in the lobby and proceeded to show them his classroom. Marcie remembered it well. They both gave Dawn a comprehensive tour of the school. Dawn was especially amazed by the technology and the kindness of the students. She

signed her way through the school, interacting with many students. They eventually made it to the cafeteria. Just before getting their food, Stephen said to them both...I have a big surprise!
I want you to meet one of my co-workers. He opened the door of the cafeteria to a small patio and asked them to wait there. He proceeded to walk across the grass, "Quadrangle", towards Brewster Gym. They could see him enter the building. He proceeded to walk down a hallway till he came to a small office.

A sign outside the door read,
"Director of Athletics.
Mr. Stephen Burns".

He poked his head inside and said, "Hey Dad, they're here". Be right there son.
The girls saw him heading back across the "Quadrangle" with another person. When they were close enough to make him out, they took off running.

Mr. Burns! ... Dad!
What are you doing here?
Girls...I work here!

Final Entreaty

Who knows where the time goes?
Who knows how my love grows?

Listen!

Amen, Amen, I say to you...

Twenty-three years ago, a young woman entered her house of worship seeking Compassion from a Merciful God. A God willing to suffer with her. He did not forsake her, but instead, took Heavenly pity on her. He chose a reluctant, personal emissary and gave him the words to say.

"Are you O.K.?"

Without a solitary word, she replied in a River of Tears. God instructed His emissary to hold her hands for Him. He already provided a "Gift" (the cassette tape) from Himself to this young Daughter of His. Little did I know... that all during the yearlong preparation for the event that produced that cassette tape that is was all about His gift to this young woman! God assured her, and all of us, that He is fully willing and able to do our "Heavy Lifting" (Falcon Heavy Lift). She was in Church making her personal plea and "*Cry*" for help.

She was at her Max-Q.

He did not abandon her! He promised all of us, including this young woman, that...

He would not...He would not... leave us "Orphans"!

I solemnly tell you; these last few sentences have been most difficult to write, as my experience with the *"silent young woman"*, transcended everything I'd ever experienced. She was suffering in ways that "words" could not convey. I have chosen to pray for her ever since.

Her tears...
her sorrowful tears,
became the inspiration for this story.

In the story, Stephen realizes, he could not pull his "Yolk" alone. His previous attempts, at going it alone, had not produced good fruit. Out of desperation... he realizes he needs different people, for different reasons, to be in his Yolk and do the "Heavy Pulling". Those persons were:

Marcie, Dawn, Katherine, Professor McBride,
Father, the Hyenas, Dean of Nursing,
and especially The Boxman and
Sister Matilda.

"Falcon Heavy...go for launch!"

Stephen needed his own personal, "Hold-Down Clamps", until he developed enough spiritual thrust to propel himself forward.

Katherine placed the palms of both
hands on his cheeks.
Stephen... it's been fun to do the impossible.
You're ready!

And, with millions of pounds of Heavenly Thrust,
his "Hold-Down Clamps" were released...
allowing him to...
"Lift-Off".

"Come to me, all you who are weary and burdened,
*and I **will** give you rest. Take my yoke upon you*
and learn from me, for I am gentle and humble
*in heart, and you **will** find rest for your souls.*
For my yoke is easy and my burden is light".

God bless every single one of my readers.
"Be good to yourselves and others!".
Rejoice in faith, all faiths.

Amen, Amen I say to you...
With God's help, it's fun to do the "Impossible"!
Can you throw someone a lifeline?
Can you please help save someone?
There are thousands of ways...pick one!

One way per The Boxman's request...

Donate to The American School for the Deaf

Composed at, "Rusatsky's Riverview", a
log cabin on the banks of the Rock River